STACY

Compilation and Introduction copyright © 2005 by
Triple Crown Publications
2959 Stelzer Rd., Suite C
Columbus, Ohio 43219
www.TripleCrownPublications.com

Library of Congress Control Number: 2005930555
ISBN# 0976789442
Cover Design/Graphics: www.MarionDesigns.com
Author: Darrell Debrew
Editor: www.phoenixblue.com
Editor in Chief: Mia McPherson
Production: Kevin J. Calloway
Consulting: Vickie M. Stringer

First Trade Paperback Edition Printing September 2005
10 9 8 7 6 5 4 3 2

Printed in the United States of America

Dedication

This book is dedicated to Linda Williams, Juan Muza (Papo) and Dolly Lopez

Acknowledgements

My most important acknowledgement goes out to Linda Williams. When a lady steps in your life and says let get this done, by all means necessary, it's time to step it up and handle yo' business like a true playa and do the right thing in all facets. Without your assistance, Linda, I would not have been able to turn this book in like I wanted to. Thank you.

My second acknowledgement goes out to Juan Muza. You hooked me up with Linda. I also have to fit Dolly Lopez in here.

To the Triple Crown family – I have to thank Vickie Stringer for the stepping stone and tolerating my everything-has-to-be-right ass. I can see us laughing about this years from now. Keep getting it on all four corners. There is no other way for a hustler. When you see Nikki Turner, thank her for Stacy and Keisha.

My man Fitzdaine Gordon – thanks for your support and I can see us making some good money in the future. You will get the first five (5) copies of Stacy as soon as it comes off the press.

To my editors – without y'alls comments and criticisms I don't think I'd be able to complete my projects. Thank you for taking out the time to read my terribly typed manuscripts: Tawan, Tank, Rodney Moss, Michael Crews, Eddie G. Jackson & Wilburn.

To my girl Phyllis Rush – I just know we are going to get together on something. Peace and Love.

I hope y'all enjoy this book.

I can be hollered at:

> Mr. Darrell James DeBrew (Da'Rel-Da'Rel)
> Reg. No 14102-056
> FCI LorettoP.O. Box 1000
> Loretto, PA 15940
>
>
> www.darrelldebrew.com

<u>Chapter One</u>

For the past twenty-four hours, Stacy Dee sat in the Philadelphia Federal Detention Center without knowing why. She had called everybody in the city and had them call everybody else, to find out what was going on. Her lawyer couldn't tell her anything or get her bail. Stacy's shit was fucked up.

Stacy held a major position in Philadelphia's most ruthless drug organization—The Untouchables. As a first-level captain she only answered to the head of the organization. She went extra hard to earn her position. Only five years ago, Stacy was strung out on heroin and supporting her habit by being a stripper and part-time prostitute. Her son caused a change in her life. Devon was the center of her existence and the source of her determination. She refused to let her life be sucked up by the streets and end up like many other females that came out of the projects; most of all, she wanted her son to see a better life.

Stacy excelled at the drug game, but had plans to get out of it with a legitimate career. Her rap single, "I'm Bangin' 'Em" was in heavy rotation all over Pennsylvania and spreading up north. In less than thirty days she was planning on passing all of her juice to her co-captain, Lisa, her favorite peeps.

"Damn this shit is fucked up! You were supposed to do that show tonight at Club Chrome," Lisa said with a tone of disappointment. She and Stacy were on yet another call.

"I'm really hurtin', girl. I'm missing my shot and I don't even know why I'm in this spot." Stacy wanted to cry because the last thing she wanted to miss was her first show. Some people from Universal and Interscope were supposed to show up and speak with her about distributing her label.

"It's going to be OK. I got everything running as smooth as a lawn mower. All the bulls are handling their business." Lisa had been with Stacy for three years. They knew everything about each other. If it weren't for Stacy, Lisa would be another single mother depending on the system or a baller to meet her needs.

"I should be out of here in a couple of hours. If they had some evidence, they would charge me by now." Stacy felt good talking to Lisa. Word on the street was that Lisa was holding it down, just as she was taught. Alvin, the headman, was extremely pleased.

"This is really crazy. Everybody is calling and asking about you. I know shit gon' be all right." Lisa tried to keep her partner's spirits up.

The word "call" made Stacy think about a question that she had asked before. "What is up with the new cell phone?" It just seemed funny that Lisa got a new cell phone a day after Stacy got locked up. The thought had been on Stacy's mind all week.

"My other cell, two-way and pager just keep blowing up with all these people calling about you. It was time for me to get a private line. I had been meaning to do it for a long time. I'm hatin' to keep answerin' my other joints because peeps are calling twenty times a day and wanting to talk to you and asking about you." There was some irritation in Lisa's voice

Stacy wasn't satisfied with the answer and was still suspicious. Anything that was unusual bothered her. Still, her partner had never shown a sign of disloyalty or jealousy. If the situation had to be called a test, she would have to give Lisa a big bonus. "A bitch can't ask a question these days?"

"It ain't that. You asked me that before. What you don't trust me? You ain't never questioned me before." From the day that Lisa got on Stacy's team she was on point, at all times. Lisa had been known to go the extra mile. For three years they had been known as "The Bitches" because that's what they called each other—nobody else was allowed—and when you saw one you saw the other.

Stacy smiled. *There was no need to be out of pocket with yo' best friend,* she thought. "You right, bitch. Close the shop for the rest of the weekend." This was a test.

"We gon' miss a lot of money," Lisa responded with suspicion.

"Are you questioning me?" Stacy growled.

"Aight."

"Take the crew out of town for about five days. This thing should be over by then. I'm not going to be calling you, and don't you call here to the city. Just party and have fun."

"Aight."

"Later, bitch, and party up."

"Later, bitch."

Back in her cell, loneliness was setting in deeper and deeper. Stacy was already lonely on the street because it was a must that she be for self. It wasn't just a matter of being that way to make it in the drug game; it was a matter of survival in South Philly. Being a female made it that much harder to attain and maintain respect in a male-dominated game. Lisa was the only person on the street that knew anything about her personal business. With a history that she couldn't escape, Stacy made sure that no man in the drug game or the music game—most cats in the music game were drug dealers—got next to her. Being called a lesbian behind her back didn't mean a thing. She knew that many of them were hoping and expecting her to fall weak. Before she put in her application Stacy made a vow that she would never fall weak and never be seen as weak, no matter what she had to do. The Ultimate Gangsta Bitch is what she called herself and many others did the same.

Every hour that she was locked up Stacy told herself that her surprise lockdown was nothing more than a test, a test that she would pass with flying colors. So far she hadn't seen another prisoner. For the first time in her life she was literally alone. She was being kept on her own tier. Most of the police that came through couldn't tell her what was going on even though she knew most of them from the streets.

"Mail call, Stacy," the guard yelled. The footsteps could be heard from down the hall. Stacy couldn't believe that she was receiving letters already. There had to about ten letters in her hand. Her mother and son sent her some cards and letters every day. There were always some from a few groupies. Stacy was shocked that there was a letter from her father.

Dear Baby Boo,

Word has reached the penitentiary that they have locked you up for no reason at all. Nobody knows anything and the rumors are spreading that you are gon' be a rat because you are a woman.

I hope that when you get this letter that you are out on bail, at the least and gettin' ready to do your show. I love it when I hear your single on the radio. You know I be gettin' my brag on. I've been tellin' the fellas that your CD is going to go double platinum.

There has never been a rat in the Dee family. Death before dishonor. Don't put me to shame.

Love, Daddy

Hearing from Dad was a good thing, but some of the news wasn't that great. When Stacy got money, her father got money. He was doing a twenty-year sentence for a murder that he had nothing to do with. His street raising wouldn't let him tell on the cats that did it. She was happy to hear from him and to hear that he was campaigning for her. The part about her being referred to as a rat—in fact, just the suggestion—was pissing her off.

If anybody were to call Stacy a rat in her presence they would pay the price immediately. Though she was only a buck and a quarter, she kept the deadliest of killers at a distance. She was known to put in work with a knife, gun or baseball bat. Her secret was to have the element of surprise; her father taught her that from the joint. There were only two men that Stacy had major respect for: her father and Alvin.

It was looking like she was going to spend the weekend in jail. Her son came to her mind when Stacy thought about getting out, which was most of the day. She knew that being locked up was hurting him the most. It was time to call him again.

"Ay," she yelled out to the male guard.

"What is it now?"

"Can I make one more phone call?"

"No it's after nine o'clock."

"Come on, please? I have to call my son and tell him goodnight."

"Did you not just hear what I said?"

"Please," Stacy begged, giving him her famous puppy dog eyes. The guard ignored her even as he wondered if he should let her or not. Glancing back at her, he caught a glimpse of her eyes again.

"OK," he said giving in. No one could resist Stacy when she gave them that look. "But only this once." He let her out the cell. Two minutes later she was on the pay phone with her son.

"Hey, Pumpkin, how's Momma's baby?"

"Momma's baby is six years old and too old to be Momma's baby." This was part of their usual dialogue.

"When you are one hundred, you are still going to be my baby."

"Well, when is my Momma going to come home?"

Stacy hated to hear him ask this question. "Real soon baby, real soon." She wished that she could tell her son the truth. She didn't want her son to know anything about the life that she led. As far as he knew she was just a recording artist.

"Momma, can I come to your concert tonight? I keep hearing them announce it over the radio. I wanna see you. I ain't seen you since Thursday." Devon was extremely proud of his mother. He loved it when he heard her song playing on the radio. He would always sing along.

"What I tell you about using the word 'ain't'?" She refused to have her son sounding like he didn't have an education.

"I'm sorry, Momma."

"Say, 'haven't seen you'." Stacy always corrected his English. She wanted him to grow up to be a lawyer or some kind of professional. Sounding gully was something Stacy wasn't going to accept from her son.

"OK Momma. I haven't seen you since Thursday. Can I come to the concert?"

Telling him that she wasn't going to be doing the concert was the last thing Stacy was going to tell him. She only hoped that he wouldn't find out. "You know you have to get yourself in the bed."

"OK, Momma. Well, at least tell me where you are at. You sure are acting funny."

"I can't do that, baby."

"When you coming home, then? You gon' be here in the morning to watch cartoons with me?" They had watched cartoons together for as long as he could remember.

"I'm going to try." A tear ran down Stacy's face. "Yes, I'm going to be there for you baby, bright and early." She couldn't help but lie. The incorrect English had slipped her attention. It was going to be the first time that she wasn't going to be there for her son—the love of her life.

"I'll see you in the morning, Ma. I love you."

"I love you, too."

Hanging up the phone, Stacy slowly walked back to her cell. Sitting on the edge of her bed she placed her face in her hands and shook her head. "Damn, damn, damn," she yelled out loud and kept yelling it over and over. Suddenly she realized how serious the game could be. In her mind Stacy was trying to figure out what was the weak link that caused her to be locked up. For her son, she had to make it out of this situation and out of the game. There was nothing worth her being separated from her Devon. Every night before she went to sleep, Stacy would think that maybe this all was a bad dream. It was the waiting without knowing what was going on, that was killing her. Having a charge and making bail would be a relief; at least she would know what was going on.

It was time for her to put it in God's hands for the sake of her son. Stacy got on her knees, propped her elbows on the bed, put her face in her palms and started to pray: "God, I know that You and I aren't on the greatest of terms. But I'm not praying for me, my freedom or my rap career. I'm praying for Devon. He's being hurt for no reason at all." Tears ran down her face.

"If You could just make it possible for me to be with my son in the morning, I'll do anything. Just please don't take me away from my son. I'm all he's got."

"God, would You do this for me?" The tears kept running as she prayed. "Walk with me back to my son. I promise to give the game up. I promise to not hurt anybody else. At this point I don't—"

"Stacy Dee, you have a visitor." Stacy was so occupied with her prayers that she hadn't heard the guard walk up to her cell.

Instinct told her that the visitor had to be a cop. No one would be visiting her on a Friday, at eight thirty at night, especially since she wasn't allowed to have any visits. "I thought that I couldn't have any visits," Stacy mumbled as she wiped her face, being careful to not let the guard see that she had been crying.

"It's a special visit."

With her hands cuffed in front of her, Stacy was led to an interrogation room. When the door was opened she didn't want to walk in because there was very little light in the room. "Go in, girl," the female guard said. "I know you want to make it to your concert tonight."

Stacy turned around and looked at her. "Ain't this a bitch," she said to herself. The expression on her face told the guard how Stacy felt about her making that comment.

"It's OK, Stacy," a male voice said. "I'm here to help you. This meeting is just between you and me only." The voice was that of an older white man with extreme confidence.

Stacy walked slowly in the room. The only light was from a small lamp that sat on a square table. On the other side of the table was a figure wearing a blue suit, white shirt and blue tie. The man's chin couldn't be seen because it was above the lamp. Though it was hard to see, Stacy looked to see if there were any other figures in the shadows.

"Have a seat, Stacy. It's only you and I. I'm here to help you. You can still make your concert, if you choose to." His deep voice let Stacy know that this cat was playing from a position of power and he knew it. She didn't want to say anything because she didn't know with whom she was dealing. "It isn't going to help for you to be silent. What you don't say is going to hurt you. I've got all the cards."

Stacy was really thinking about making the concert. It meant a lot to her. All week she had been hoping that she would be able to get bond and make it to the concert. "Aren't you supposed to read me my rights or something?" She was trying to be a participant without assisting the police. She made her comment because she knew for sure that the bull was a cop and that cops have rules to follow that respected her rights—though she didn't exactly know her rights.

"Well, they said that you were smart and tough. In certain ways that'll make things easier for both of us." He wanted to take his time in getting to the point. "You see, you aren't under arrest yet, and this isn't an interrogation. In fact, I don't have to interrogate you. I know all that I need to know to keep you locked up."

Though Stacy didn't know what he was talking about, she could tell by the sound of his voice that he was dead serious and deadly. She wanted to ask him if he was the Grim Reaper. "Since you know so much about me, why don't you just go on and convict me?"

"Like I said, I want to help you help yourself."

"I'm just a schoolgirl that is trying to make it."

"Yes, you are. You do go to school part-time. But you hustle heroin and cocaine on a full-time basis for The Untouchables." He laughed in an arrogant manner that was meant to scare her a bit.

Stacy couldn't help but squint her eyes; she didn't realize that this told the man that he was getting to her. "I don't know what you talkin' about. Who would lie on me like that?" Stacy heard the defensiveness in her response and winced again. No matter, it might help to get the response that she was looking for.

"You are right." The man laughed again. "No one has lied on

you. We know it's all true because we have enough evidence. Plus, we've been listening to all of your phone calls. Your friends don't know how to talk on the phone. We've been giving you plenty of rope to hang yourself."

Stacy had also been thinking the same thing about her friends' telephone manners. Her palms began to sweat. What the fuck was going on? "You act like you caught me with some drugs or something." She wasn't the type to give in and give up her slightly innocent front. Might as well play the game as far as it would go.

The man smirked and laughed. He had heard the same thing from every defendant that was charged, or was about to be charged, with a drug conspiracy. "I don't have to catch you with anything. I'm part of the federal government. We do things differently from the State of Pennsylvania."

"Well, at least I know that you're a Fed. Now can you charge me and let me beat the charge." She felt a bit more powerful now that she knew with whom she was dealing.

"Oh no, my dear. It isn't going to be that easy for you. You aren't going to beat the charge; I'm going to make sure of that."

"What are you talking about?"

"When we get through, you'll wish that you had gotten caught with the drugs." A silly smirk was on his face.

"If your threats are so good, then why don't you give me bail?" It made Stacy feel good to ask him some good questions that would help her get some answers.

He laughed again. "You won't be making bail. Unless you work with me, you won't be seeing the streets ever again."

Stacy sucked her teeth before he could finish his sentence. "Let me get this straight. You haven't caught me with any drugs, but you are going to convict me for drugs." She sucked her teeth again and waved her hand in dismissal. "You must be out your mind. So when you charge me, I'm not going to get a bail. Then I'm not going to see the streets again."

"You basically got it, except the part about helping yourself. And in case you need to know, it's called a conspiracy."

"What?"

"It's called a conspiracy. All we need are pictures, tapes and a witness."

"I don't know where you're going to get that from, especially a witness to lie on me. I don't sell drugs." Stacy knew that cats were scared to testify about The Untouchables. It had been like that for years.

"We've been finishing up. We had to take you off the streets so that people wouldn't be scared to testify."

It sounded like some silly shit to her and a bluff. "Do what you got to do, then."

"So you don't want to help yourself? I just need you to testify on one cat." He really meant a few cats.

"I'm not trying to hear it."

"All you have to do is sign a statement and you can walk out of here, right now." Stacy's signature would immediately make her a rat. If she changed her mind afterwards, they would threaten to make copies of the document for the streets. It's a game that hadn't failed the Feds yet.

"I'm not trying to hear it."

"All those record companies are going to be at your concert."

"Humph, whatever."

"OK. You'll never see the streets again as a free woman."

"Look I ain't trying to hear that bullshit. Do what you got to do and leave me the fuck alone."

"Feisty, huh? Soon you'll be trying to hear what I'm talking about when you see how I put in work. That is how y'all say it, right? As of now, you'll be charged with conspiracy." He turned off the lamp and walked out of the room through an unseen door. He figured that Stacy was going to give in. This was just the beginning of the pressure that would be put on her. When the door slammed behind him, the other officer opened the door and took Stacy back to her cell.

Chapter Two

The Untouchables were having an emergency meeting to talk about Stacy Dee's situation. They were in the back of Club Beyond, in downtown Philly.

"This shit with Stacy is probably about to get real serious," Alvin said to start the meeting. "We are going to have to prepare for the worst."

"Yeah," Tyrone agreed. "That broad is going to bring down The Untouchables." Tyrone was a captain. He tried his best to keep Stacy as a lieutenant, mainly because she wouldn't give him any pussy. If he hadn't been speaking with Alvin he would have straight out called her a bitch and a possible rat. Tyrone was used to intimidating people because he was dark- skinned, six-two and two seventy-five.

As usual, Alvin was the wise and worthy old head. He was still all of that, though he was in a wheelchair at the age of fifty. "Stacy is as true to the game as any cat in this room." Stacy was like a daughter to him and all knew it.

"Listen here, Alvin," Jimmy said in a laid back voice to show respect. He was the gentleman of the group. "We all know that the Feds are going after her because she's a female. The girl just got it all together a few years ago. We can't forget that she's a woman, with a child and a potentially lucrative rap career on the bud. What are you going to say if she decides to go to the grand jury on us?"

"It ain't gon' happen. She knows the price. I know that girl."

"We are going to have to look at our options." Quadir was usually the last one to put his piece in. He liked for everybody else to put their views on the table, so he could have a better position from where to argue. He was next in line after Alvin. Quadir wanted Alvin's position, but he didn't want to do a twenty-five-year bid to get it. "We can make this real simple. We'll just hold her mother and son until the situation is resolved. And if she makes the wrong move, we'll hold you responsible, Alvin." At thirty-five, Quadir was the second oldest in the crew. He was known to be sinister, quiet, scheming and manipulative. He liked and respected Stacy. Regardless, he had to get his.

Alvin's eyes turned blood red. "What the fuck is all of this about?" He turned his wheelchair toward Quadir. "You can save that bullshit for the people that work for you. I can still make you a lieutenant." Alvin was planning to die at the top, of natural causes. Quadir kept Alvin frustrated—one day he was with him, the next he was against him; one day he loved Stacy like a sister, the next day he hated her like they had just gotten a divorce or just because she was female.

Quadir looked at Alvin in a way that let him know that he was not threatened. Everybody knew that Quadir had people that would do whatever he said and whenever he said it. Sooner or later people figured that Quadir was gon' get up the nerve to take Alvin out and take his position. For now, he was trying to have his way and keep the peace. "Look, I'm trying to do what's best for The Untouchables."

"I'm down for kidnapping the kid and mother," Tyrone commented. "We'll turn them loose when things are cool."

Jimmy burst out, "That's fair." He didn't think about the fact that just the kidnapping itself was disrespecting Stacy. If it were him, he would feel highly disrespected.

Quadir was feeling rather good inside because he had said the right thing at the right time. Like a true general, he was thinking about his next move. A triple kidnapping of Alvin and his two bodyguards might work well with the chaos at hand.

"No," Alvin hollered as he banged his fist on the table. It was unusual for him to act this mad. He wasn't going to let anybody kidnap his godson.

"So what are we supposed to do?" Quadir stated. With a stone face, deep voice and mustache Quadir could have been mistaken for Malcolm X in a kufi. Seldom did he lose his cool. He had so much respect in the streets that few dared to argue with him. Many had just disappeared without a trace for saying the wrong thing in the wrong way. All knew what happened, but nobody really knew.

Jimmy wanted to say that it was wrong for Quadir to argue with Alvin about Stacy. Stacy was their equal and Alvin was the boss that had kept them out of prison for over ten years.

"We are going to give her the respect that we would want for ourselves if one of us was in the same position. My lawyers are going to keep up with what's happening. Meeting adjourned."

Jimmy wanted to say that that's the way it should be. As the person that usually was the peacemaker, he knew it was best that he didn't say anything. But he had to make eye contact with Alvin to indicate that he was fully with him and that he was sorry for what he had just said earlier. When their eyes met, Alvin knew what Jimmy was feeling and Jimmy knew that Alvin understood.

The headman had spoken and with logic, like any great leader should. So that was that. Quadir was one to never argue with logic that was sound. He knew that he would have felt highly disrespected for someone even thinking that he would be a rat. But was it really over?

* * * *

It was two a.m. when Stacy woke up. She couldn't get out of her head what the federal agent had told her. There was no missing link that she could think of. There were few that were close enough to her to do real damage. None of them had shown any signs of weakness that she could see. Now that she knew that the Feds were on her back, and she had been charged with conspiracy, she couldn't wait to talk to her lawyer, in person. That was the only person that was allowed to visit her. It would be Sunday before her attorney was coming back though.

Stacy needed to know if this federal cat could do all that he said that he could do. The only thing Alvin could tell her, when she called him, was that the Feds were known to be nasty and for making people turn against each other by breaking them down. She knew that Alvin was in her corner, though he sounded like he was sick. He was the one that had sent her the cell phone and other things to make her feel comfortable after she had only been there for a day. He didn't want her to call him on the prison phone. To her, and to everybody else, Alvin was always some steps ahead of the game. This time, it seemed he wasn't even with the game.

Her song came on the radio. It hurt Stacy to her heart that she couldn't do her first concert. Deep in her gut the pain ran and turned up a few levels as she thought about the worse case scenario—doing life in prison like the federal agent had talked about. She wanted to holler out that it just wasn't fair. She knew that if she were a man, she wouldn't be tested like this. Torture was the only thing that she could really call it. All signs told her that things were about to get really rough. The tears wouldn't stop running down her pretty, perfectly rounded, dark caramel-colored cheeks.

Stacy was still ready to fight. She was looking forward to having a serious battle with the Feds and whoever was giving information on her. The weak link had to be found. Stacy was used to being challenged, especially by men. She hadn't lost a battle yet and wasn't planning on losing this one and going out like the weak bitch that many wished that she were. It was on and poppin'. *There ain't no rules when the rules are broken*, she thought, because it had to be somebody that she been good to, as she cried herself to sleep.

* * * *

Sunday, April 19

"Damn, Jalissa," was the way Stacy started the conversation with her lawyer. "I didn't think that you were going to make it." Jalissa was supposed to have been there by twelve p.m. It was now three p.m.

"Baby girl, it's Sunday and I have a son, just like you." Jalissa and Stacy could have passed for sisters—same complexion, same length hair and same smile. When they were strippers together some mistook them for twins, especially when they dressed alike. Stacy, unlike Jalissa, didn't get her hair done when she was in Philadelphia. She just kept her hair pulled straight back in a ponytail. "That Fed bull was talking some serious shit when he came to see me." Stacy wanted some answers and she wanted them quick.

"What exactly did he tell you?" Jalissa was used to her clients being excited when they first encountered the Feds.

"He said that he knew everything about me, that I wouldn't be making bail, that I would never be seeing the streets again if I didn't help him. You know I ain't no rat bitch, so I stayed quiet. Then the muthafucker charged me with conspiracy."

"Girl, I'm going to keep it real with ya, like I always do." Jalissa had used her stripper earnings to support her son and earn a law degree. She hadn't forgotten the 'hood. "The Feds have probably picked you as the weak link to get The Untouchables."

"So why did they take so long to charge me?

"They really don't want you. They want you to be the snitch.

All the pressure they can come up with is going to be used, especially in a special case like this one." Jalissa was in full lawyer mode and knew that Stacy would appreciate it that she kept it real all the way, no matter what was being faced.

"What you mean, in a special case like this?" Stacy was hoping to hear some good news. Shit wasn't sounding too good right now.

"I'm going to be straight with you." Jalissa was hoping that she wouldn't scare her partner to the point that she would want to be a rat. All respect would be lost. "The Feds are going to break all the rules because they know they can get away with it. You could have easily walked out of here after twenty-four hours because you hadn't been charged with a crime. We all know that they aren't supposed to just hold you like this. In the end, the courts will just rule that it was harmless error."

"Shit." Stacy was pissed. Jalissa was talking like all of this was normal and Stacy hated it because she knew she had no choice but to believe her. "Well, what the fuck can you do?" There was much frustration in her voice.

"We got to find a weak link in the case, if there is one." Because of how hard it was to beat the Feds she didn't want to get her client overexcited. "If we find a weak link, we might be able to beat this motherfucker." This was the best thing Jalissa could say without lying. Nothing would make her lie to her homegirl. They had been through too much together.

"I can't believe that there is a weak link in our organization or my game. All of our people are strong and dependable."

"They be bluffin' sometimes." Jalissa had seen the baddest of the toughest tell on the whole crew. "But we ain't gon' know until they make their next move. What was the guy's name, and what agency did he say that he was with?"

"Damn, I was so pissed that I didn't ask him any of that. He just kept telling me that all I needed to do was promise to help them—then I could go and do my concert."

"Usually they pick up all the people they can and wait to see whose going to be the first to break." She knew that her girl wasn't going to be a rat, so she was able to skip that part of the conversation, though she was obligated to explain the benefits.

"OK, the Feds play on the gully level. Can't you file something to get me out of here?

"Since they've charged you with conspiracy that means that A, they have witness and B, they have some bogus drugs that they're going to use to pen you. If I press the U.S. Attorney's office, they'll say that they don't know what the fuck is going on. All of the federal agencies are going to say the same thing."

"So they are just playing a game with me?" Stacy was thinking to herself what kind of games she was going to play with the snitch.

"I hate to say it." Jalissa knew that at all times she had to think like a cop and a prosecutor to be a good lawyer.

"So I'm just sitting here in limbo?" Stacy's voice had become coarser. Stacy drove at every angle that she could think of. Though she didn't like the answers, she had to accept reality. Jalissa convinced her to look at the good side—until there was a charge, the whole thing could be looked upon as a major bluff move. Stacy hadn't done any hard time before and wondered, could she really go through it? After a minute she felt that she should be ashamed to complain about doing a few days in jail, when her father had already served twenty years for a murder that he hadn't committed. Just look at the situation as a needed vacation, was Stacy's decision to view it.

Stacy was still mad that she had missed cartoons with her son. Making it up to him was the only thing that she could do. One day he would understand, she hoped.

"So what took you so long to answer the phone? It rang eight times," Stacy hollered into the phone when Jesse picked up.

"For real, it's about time that you called a dude. It's only been six days since yo' ass been locked up. I don't believe that you believe that I have feelings." Jesse was her accountant, financial advisor and so-called boyfriend—really, gigolo.

"I didn't call you to tell me what I already know. I need to know if you've been missing me." This is how they usually started out their phone conversations.

"You know I miss you."

"Well, say my name and tell me what you miss about me." Stacy acted like she was jealous to feed Jesse's ego. All she really cared about was that he was a really good handler of money and a dependable booty call when she was stressed. At times she wished that he would make her respect him more.

"I miss you, Stacy Dee, and I miss that good-ass pussy of yours." Jesse was a natural-born ass-kisser. He was deeply in love with Stacy Dee and would do anything that she demanded.

"If you miss me so much, why haven't you sent me a card or something? A little letter would have been nice. What, you can't figure out the address? Or you didn't know where I was because you don't watch the news or listen to the radio. Or you hadn't checked on my whereabouts." Without being soft, Stacy always spoke her mind. Jesse was perfect for her lifestyle and needs. She only hoped that he wouldn't continue to play a role for her. It didn't matter to her that they spent her money when they went places, she still wanted more aggressiveness from him.

"Well, you could give it to me," he replied in an easy tone, like he was just saying it because it was the right thing to say without being disrespectful. He figured that no matter what he did, Stacy was going complain. He just decided to let her yank his chain before he barked. He was planning on telling her how much he loved her, one day.

"You're an accountant. You figure it out." Stacy wanted to see if he could stand up to her under the circumstances. She knew that he had it in him.

"When are you getting out? And why are they holding you?" Jesse usually changed the subject when she was spazzin' off. In the back of his mind, he thought he would lose Stacy if he spoke his mind and tried to put her in check. Jesse didn't mind her temperament, as long as she didn't embarrass him in front of anybody. When they'd visited places like New York, California, France and Canada she acted like a perfect lady and footed the bill, along with putting a few dollars in his pocket. The Rolex didn't hurt matters either. In Philadelphia, where they were seldom seen together, Jesse figured he could stand it.

"Shit ain't looking good. I got charged with a conspiracy case. I got to go, the guard is coming. Bye." Stacy heard footsteps approaching.

"Stacy, you have a visitor."

"Who the hell is it?"

"It's the same guy."

Triple Crown Publications presents

<u>**Chapter Three**</u>

When Stacy got to the door this time she wasn't scared or hesitant to walk in. She was prepared to play.

The federal agent was wearing a black suit, a crisp, freshly starched white shirt and a jet black tie. The dark sunglasses and the black hat gave him a Blues Brothers look. "I hope you've been thinking about your freedom." He was speaking slowly and deliberately, like he wanted her to hear every syllable.

"Of course I've been thinking about my freedom." She was being nice so that she could eventually get his name and the agency he worked for.

"Because if you give us some information on The Untouchables, we'll drop the conspiracy charges. I heard through the grapevine that several labels want to give you a distribution deal. My sources are reliable." He was talking so slow and with so much bass in his voice, that it was almost irritating and condescending.

Smiling was what Stacy didn't want to do, though her mood had changed totally. She couldn't resist showing how pleased she was to hear what he just said.

"So that makes you happy, huh?"

"OK, you got me on that."

"We really don't want to keep you here, my dear. We want the members of The Untouchables."

"Well, who are you and who is we?"

The man tapped his fingers on the table. "You just need to know that we want to take you before the grand jury. We can give you and your family protection and immunity. You'll have bodyguards around the clock while you are on tour." He had chosen a weak spot and planned to keep driving at it.

"That's really nice of you, but I'm not the one." Stacy was on her best behavior.

He tapped his fingers faster. "We know all about you. We know about what you did to Patrick. We know all the details."

She tried to act surprised. "Who is Patrick?" Her heart rate sped up. Only The Untouchables knew for sure what had happened to Patrick. Lisa also knew because she had been told. There was no way that Stacy was going to believe that someone in The Untouchables had turned bad, or that Lisa had betrayed her. She talked to Lisa every single day. Plus, Lisa was now out of town.

"Patrick is the guy that stole twenty ounces of heroin." He was waiting to get a reaction. Later on he was going to study the tape of this meeting until he knew when Stacy was lying or telling the truth.

Damn, he's almost on point, Stacy thought. "I don't know what the fuck you are talking about." The more he talked and tapped his fingers the more she wanted to scream. What the fuck is really going on?

"We are going to serve you with a sealed indictment next week. After that, you aren't going to be able to save yourself." He spoke faster because he knew he was getting to her.

Stacy tried to sit still, but it was getting harder and harder. "I can't help you."

"A beautiful twenty-three year old with a life sentence. We are going to be extremely careful so that you can't get back on appeal." He laughed his funny laugh.

"You got the wrong chick."

"Your son is going to grow up without you, just like you grew up without your father."

"What the fuck does my father have to do with this?" Stacy couldn't take it. He was on sacred ground.

This excited the agent. He laughed really hard. "We can give him a money-laundering charge because of all the money that you sent him. We have copies of all the letters you wrote him and all the letters he wrote you." He was bluffing about the letters but it sounded so good that he had to throw it in. He loved his job.

What do I say? What do I do? What the fuck is going on? Is this shit really this deep? Are they really on me like that? Stacy had begun to sweat and grit her teeth. She didn't want her father to catch a federal case. He was just about to max out his sentence.

"Yeah, little girl. This shit is that deep. You are going to be the only one from The Untouchables that's going to be in jail, with a life sentence. Life means life in the Feds."

This motherfucker is dead serious about doing me in, Stacy said to herself. She thought about jumping across the table and attacking him.

"Everybody else from The Untouchables is still going to be on the street making money, driving fancy cars and fucking everything. You'll be serving time for them. Do you think that they would do it for you?"

Instead of spitting venom like she wanted to, Stacy kept quiet. Being the prey was something she hadn't experienced in a long time. She refused to lose the thing that she could always control—herself. There was nothing that she could say that would be correct. She was tired of repeating "no" in one form or another. When she got back to her cell she was numb and couldn't get to sleep. She wanted to take an evening nap before dinner was served so she could wake up fresh and think clearly. She had to admit to herself that she was shaken. Would the rest of The Untouchables do the time without telling on her, she wondered. She was beginning to see that being hard and going up against the Feds by herself wasn't going to be an easy task. The shit the Feds were talking was real and her small cell seemed to be getting smaller and smaller.

When she turned on her radio her song was playing:

I'm bangin' 'em

That's what I do

I'm bangin' 'em

Ooh, ooh, ooh,

I'm bangin' 'em

That's what I do

Get my money, fool!

"Damn," Stacy cried out as she threw her radio and headphones against the wall.

"Yo Stacy," the female guard whispered, catching her attention.

Looking down on the ground Stacy saw that a cell phone had been slid through the bars. Rushing over she hurried and placed the cell phone into her pocket.

"Thank you," Stacy whispered back.

Still vexed, she wanted to take off the ugly blue uniform[TMD1] that she wore and tear it into shreds to relieve some of the tension she was feeling. There was no way she was going to let them know that the pressure was getting to her. Instead, she started pacing and trying to figure a way up out of the situation. Stacy refused to go down like a rat—her pride and determination would never allow her to spit on her name. She also refused to go down because of a rat, if she could help it.

* * * *

Jimmy was the last one to get to the café. "What is this emergency meeting about? We just had an emergency meeting yesterday."

"Why are you always the last one to arrive? You are always late." Quadir stayed in Jimmy's shit because he could use these things to maintain control and get his way. He was using his I'm-bigger-and-better-than-you voice.

"I'm not last. Alvin isn't here."

"Alvin wasn't invited to this meeting," Tyrone growled.

Jimmy was the real fly guy of the group. Pretty boy he was, punk he wasn't. "That's rather treacherous. This must have been your idea, Quadir," he stated as he slid in the booth to the left of Quadir. He knew that something was really up because of the look on Tyrone's face.

"Yes, this was my idea and I'm doing what is best for The Untouchables. It's a now or never situation." Quadir cut his eyes at Jimmy after he made the statement.

"Yeah, it's a now or never situation," Tyrone repeated. His eyes looked like they were about to jump out of his head.

"What the fuck are y'all talkin' about? Y'all got to be on somethin'." When he got the call from Tyrone and Tyrone told him to not make any other calls and that Al said so, Jimmy's instincts told him that something was wrong. Al had never told him not to make any phone calls.

Quadir let out a deep breath like what he was going to say was going to be difficult to get out. "We got to make a move. Shit is about to get real serious. All of Stacy's people dipped over the weekend. Nobody knows where they are at. We can't even find Lisa." He hadn't tried to find anybody.

"So, what that mean?"

"That means the Feds are getting ready to start busting down doors." Quadir practically had all of his answers planned.

"So what else does that mean?" Jimmy had known Quadir since the seventh grade. He knew there was much more.

"That means that Stacy may be protecting her people so she can do us and our people."

"Get the fuck out of here! Stacy ain't no snitch! She harder than Gangsta Boo and you know it." Though Stacy wouldn't give Jimmy any play, he treated her like his little sister.

Tyrone simply looked back and forth. All it took was a few drinks and a little bit of talk to sell him a dream. Quadir had him in check.

"Listen, tomorrow will make a week that the girl has been off the streets. We don't even know for sure that she's in the detention center." Quadir thumped his finger on the table. "We don't know where her crew is at." He thumped his finger on the table again. "We don't know where her head L.T. is at," he thumped. "We only know what she's been telling us on the phone, and the phone could be tapped." He banged his fist.

"So what are we supposed to do?" Jimmy knew it was best to get to the point, then argue from there. He could also see that Tyrone was already wrapped around Quadir's finger.

"We got to buy some insurance. Some real good insurance that'll keep her mouth shut. We're The Untouchables. We need to remain that way. We ain't going down."

"You still ain't said what we supposed to be doing. Quit beating around the bush and shit. Wit' your ol' Malcolm X, Louis Farrakhan, wanna-be ass."

"Fuck you nigga! It's her or us. I know yo' punk ass ain't tryin' to get locked up." Their eyes were locked.

"She's a part of us, and has been for the longest motherfuckin' time. Plus, Al has a say in this matter. Why ain't he here?"

"We both know that Al has an emotional attachment to that girl. He's probably fucking her."

"I bet you won't let him hear you say that."

Tyrone wanted them to hurry up and get to the point of the meeting.

"That's why Al ain't here. He don't know what the fuck is the best for us when it comes to that girl. She used to be a dopehead and probably still is, undercover."

"If she is, she ain't the only one in the crew that be getting high on the regular." Tyrone had been getting busy, heavily, on the regular. A broad broke his heart about a year ago, which got him into taking drugs. His habit was so large that he owed money to everybody in the crew.

"So, what the fuck is that supposed to mean?" Tyrone hollered. Some people in the café started to look around.

"It means that y'all are trying to treat the girl like she don't deserve some respect. This shit is fucked up. And you doing the shit behind Al's back."

"Look Jimmy," Quadir responded as he grabbed Jimmy's forearm. Jimmy snatched it away. "This is about survival. We know the Feds got that girl. The state don't play this dirty. I can't sit back and wait. The minimum sentence that we'll be getting is life. They not gon' treat us no better than the other crews. They been at The Untouchables for over twenty years."

"OK. You already said that part. What are we supposed to do?"

Quadir knew this was going to be the hard part with Jimmy. "We got to leave the state forever, or kidnap her son and mother." The last part was said in a lower tone.

"What the fuck is wrong with you? I ain't ready to leave and I ain't gon' do no kidnapping concerning a crewmember's relatives. We don't even know where they stay." If Jimmy really had to choose, he would leave the state, though he really didn't want to be on the run. He knew that his money wouldn't last him more than a few months. He was known to blow $50,000 in a week's time without a problem.

Tyrone already knew that dipping was out of the question for him. He was already in debt from gambling and supporting his heroin habit. The gambling was the real problem. All he knew was Philadelphia. And the only way he knew how to get money was drugs. He had always spent money as fast as he made it or faster. He owed Quadir close to a million dollars for bailing him out all the time. He was like Quadir's son. Quadir didn't mind because he knew he would get it back just for having Tyrone support whatever he did.

"Point blank, I ain't going down unless I have to. It's either we go to a country that won't extradite us or we get some insurance." Quadir was prepared to go in either direction but his mind was already made up, and he wasn't going to take no for an answer.

"I'm out of here." Jimmy hollered, as he rose up from the table.

Quadir grabbed him by the arm and wouldn't let go. "Hear me out, baby boy. If you walk out that door without me, you won't make it down the block."

"Nah, my nigga, don't even take your As-salaamu-alaikium ass there. Don't you know who you are threatening?"

Tyrone was hoping that it wouldn't come down to this. They were all like brothers.

"Man, you know that I don't want to, but I had to. It's for our own good. Later, you will see."

Jimmy could sense by the tone of his voice and the look in his eyes that Quadir wasn't bluffing. Plus, Jimmy knew that Quadir wasn't a good bluffer and it showed doing the few times he played poker. "OK. I'm with you. But if you threaten me again, one of us is gon' die."

"I'm sorry, my brother. If we're wrong, we'll apologize to Stacy. We aren't going to harm them, just hold them."

Tyrone was satisfied. Jimmy felt like he had been played. Quadir was out to get it all with his diabolical mind.

Chapter Four

Waking up from her nap, Stacy felt a little rested and refreshed. What the mysterious Fed cat had said to her was just too much. Pulling her cell phone from underneath the pillow, she began to make a call.

"What's going on baby? I've been waiting..."

"Alvin, shit ain't good," Stacy cut him off.

"Just calm down."

In a nearby room, federal agents listened to the tapped phone call.

"I hope we are getting all of this on tape," The fed agent said to his assistant.

"We are going to break this bitch — then break The Untouchables." He laughed and smiled as he listened to Stacy and Alvin.

"When are we going to drop the indictment on her?" the assistant asked.

"Just as soon as our rat gets us a little more evidence."

Meanwhile, Alvin continued to try to calm Stacy down.

"Them motherfuckers can't know as much as you say they know." Alvin was trying to figure out the best thing to do. Panicking wasn't the best option.

"I'm telling you that we need to find the rat before it's too late! I know this federal motherfucker isn't playing games." Stacy was frantic and talking unusually loud.

"You got to calm down. We just going through some rough times."

"Just keep talking, Alvin," the federal agent sneered. "The more you talk, the easier it's going to be to put you in the conspiracy, whoever you are. We might not need her to snitch. I could get y'all tried side by side."

"What about the rest of the top people?"

"Uhm, that's a good question. Shit, might as well put them on the indictment and take them to trial also. One of them might snitch."

"I can't go out like this, Alvin. If I'm going down, I'm going down fighting. I can't stand to have my son visiting me in prison, you understand?"

"Listen. I understand that you are scared. I really do. We all know that the Feds don't play and they don't play fair."

"Yes, I can see it now. I've been trying to get these cats for almost a decade. Boom! The right person called my office and it's almost over for them. Ha, ha, ha."

"So why are we waiting before we pick them up?"

"The longer she sits in that cell, the more evidence we get. I can't take any chances. I think she's about to break."

"What part of the game is this, Al?" Stacy was still yelling. "You never told me that after twenty-four hours I could've been released! They held me hostage for three fucking days without me even knowing!"

"You're right, Stacy; we'll just say there was a mix-up with the paperwork."

"It's a dirty game." They both laughed.

"Damn, girl! You ain't never talked this much at one time. Save some of that shit for your next album." Alvin wanted to hang up the phone, but Stacy was special to him.

"There isn't going to be a next album, if what this cat is spittin' is true. There ain't gon' be nothin' but me getting lots of time for my crew." That rhymes, she thought.

"You see what I'm talking about? A few more days and she'll be ready to break. Plus, we don't know what Alvin looks like or anything."

"I'm willing to bet there are pictures of her and Alvin together somewhere."

"You might have a point."

"There is no way that you can know how I feel. Your ass isn't locked up."

"OK, I get the point. I'm going to get you out of this and out of there." Under normal circumstances, Alvin wouldn't have allowed anybody to talk to him like that or in that tone.

"You better. You're supposed to be protectin' me. Bye." Click.

Stacy thought to herself, before she went back to sleep, that maybe she shouldn't have been that hard on Alvin. There was a possibility that the fed cat could be straight bluffing and seeing how long it would take for her to crack. On the other hand, she was a celebrity and she knew the media was keeping up with her. Would the Feds just violate her rights right in front of the world? Nothing that she thought seemed to make sense. There was little she could do, except make phone calls. This made her feel powerless and vulnerable – the feelings she hated the most because they reminded her of her old profession, which is how she met Alvin. All she could do was depend on Alvin and write her father.

Dear Daddy,

It is bad. I mean bad as in bad. I don't know if I am going to make it. I'm trying to be strong but this sitting and waiting shit is killing me. But I'm gon' keep it gangsta for you and Devon.

Love, Stacy

* * * *

Wednesday, April 23

Nothing had changed. Stacy started having shit brought in to make her stay more comfortable. She just knew that she was waiting for several things to happen: getting arrested, Al getting her out, Lisa getting back in town or for the federal agent to come back and scare her again. Her poster of the rapper Eve kept her focused on writing rhymes. Might as well get started on the next album, she thought.

Stacy cut straight into Lisa when she heard her voice. "Your ass has been back in town since twelve o'clock. That was six hours ago. Where the fuck have you been and why haven't you been answering your phone?"

Lisa hadn't answered any of her calls since she had gone to Cancún on vacation.

"I've been taking care of some business. Can't a bitch take care of a bitch?" Lisa yelled back. She thought that her partner would be happy to hear her voice.

"I just told you to go out of town. I didn't tell you to not keep in touch."

"My cell phone wasn't going to work in Cancún. At least, I don't think it was." Lisa was really tired of getting all those calls, so she left her phone, beeper and two-way at home. "When the fuck are you getting out?"

Stacy had calmed a little bit. "Nothing has changed. I'm sorry for blowing up at you. It's just that I've been wanting to talk to you."

"Girl, I wish you could have been with us. There were some fly-ass Mexican guys down there. I was with one of them for about three days." Lisa intentionally wanted Stacy to get her mind off distrusting her. She was tired of being questioned, especially after all the loyalty she had shown from day one.

"Now there you go with your fast ass, bitch. That's why you got all those kids." Stacy wanted to mention the three baby daddies but since that made Lisa mad, she didn't.

"The dick was as good as a motherfucker. I told him to fuck me nice and easy, just the way I like it. Then I told him to fuck the hell out of me like he was going crazy. He did that too."

"Yeah, bitch."

"On the third day I had him calling my name out loud. Pedro was telling me that he wanted to marry me and come live with me in the States." Lisa lied about that part.

"Yeah, bitch! So what else happened?"

"On the fourth day he told me that his wife was going to kill him if she caught us together. I just think he wanted to get a green card."

"Stop lying, bitch."

"No shit. The Mexican dick was good as a motherfucker. You got to come next time and get you some."

"You know better, bitch."

"You know you need some right now. If I was in there all alone, I know my pussy would be wet, drippin' and throbbin'." Lisa loved to talk about men. She wasn't good-looking enough to attract the ones that she wanted. Most guys that approached her asked about Stacy.

"Bitch, your ass gon' catch something one of these days." Stacy wasn't with fucking around. One man was enough.

"See bitch, there you go, wishin' a bitch bad luck. I need to get my game as tight as yours so I can have a dick all to myself."

"They know too much, baby girl!!!" Stacy's tone and attitude changed.

"What did you say?" Lisa hated it when she did that.

"They know too much." She said it in a much more serious tone.

"Damn girl, we was ridin'."

"Shit too serious. The Feds came to see me."

"When are they going to charge you?" Lisa had to take a dutiful interest, though she didn't want to talk about this at the moment.

"The same guy came to see me twice and he knows a lot of shit." Stacy didn't want to talk to her ace like she was a suspect, but all were suspects, until proven differently.

"Listen, you my bitch and that means we gon' talk like we always done. These phones that we have can't be tapped because they're brand new. So tell me the deal."

Lisa always seemed to know how to make her feel better. The phones being brand new now meant something. "He brung up Patrick's name. Says he knows it was about some heroin."

"Girl, you got to be playing."

"I wouldn't play with ya' like that."

"Our whole crew has been in Cancun, so you can count us out as information centers."

"I'm just tellin' you what's happenin'. I'm not tryin' to blame anyone. Though I want to know because the *federales* is talking about giving me life for Patrick. I got to find the rat. *We* got to find the rat."

"Yeah, we got to find the rat. I'm with you, bitch."

Hanging up the phone, for the first time in over a week Stacy was reminded of the fact that she hadn't gotten dicked down in a while. Hearing Lisa brag about her sexual escapades in Cancún had Stacy hornier than a muthafucker. Sliding her dress up she placed her fingers inside of her panties and slowly began to massage her clit. Thinking of Jesse, she reminisced on how he used to thumb her clit and then lick the pussy.

Rubbing her breasts, she pretended as if it were Jesse's hand that was doing all the work. Wet and fully aroused, she felt an orgasm coming on. Rotating her fingers faster Stacy arched her back and prepared to cum. Wanting to scream out Jesse's name, but remembering where she was, Stacy bit down onto her bottom lip as cum juices soaked her fingers.

Now that was a good nut.

* * * *

Thursday, April 24
Stacy was feeling much better since her girl was back in town and on the job to find the rat. She had eaten lunch and gotten comfortable on her bunk, so that she could write some more rhymes. With her headphones on, pen in right hand and writing pad resting on her lap, she was waiting for a song with a good beat to get her creative juices flowing. Stacy just needed some incense to go along with her Eve poster and she would feel like she could do a few more days in the spot, if necessary.

A slow song had just finished playing before Stacy heard the deejay speak. "Just in over the hotwires," the deejay spat, as usual, before he put out the latest and hottest news. "Stacy Dee, Philadelphia's hottest female rapper, has just been indicted by the federal government." Stacy's mouth dropped open. "One of the main charges is for the murder of Patrick Allison. Another rapper's career might go down the drain because of the street life."

"Damn, damn, damn! Eve, this shit is fucked up. This shit is for real." The first thing she did was try to call Alvin. There was no answer, so she called Lisa. "Girl, a bitch just got indicted!" Stacy didn't speak in an angry or disgusted tone. She just needed to tell somebody.

"Don't this mean that a bitch can get a bond?"

"Damn, bitch. That's what the fuck I love about your ass. You be thinkin'." Lisa was that close to Stacy because she always made herself useful and dependable and could keep a secret.

"Yeah, bitch. The first thing that we have to do is reschedule your show." As usual, Lisa was doing some major thinking for Stacy and keepin' Stacy's mental together.

"I love you, bitch."

"I love you too, bitch."

"I got to call my lawyer." *Click.*

OK, the *federale* bull wasn't bluffin' — or so it seemed. Stacy lay on her bunk to do some major thinking. The more she thought about it, being indicted wasn't that bad; in fact, because of the circumstances, she was relieved to be taken out of suspense. Now she could get bail. No matter the bail amount, she knew that Alvin was coming to get her, even if it was $5,000,000 in cash. Now that she had a case and was about to make bail, it would be time to take care of what was going to be the most important part of the federal case — find the rat and put the rat out of commission. Stacy smiled to herself while she was looking up at the ceiling. "I'm that Gangster Bitch, and I'm not going out like a sucker. The rat must die," she said out loud, with conviction, like she had a crowd of people around her.

* * * *

It took Jimmy, Quadir and Tyrone almost three hours before they ran Alvin down. He was in the back of one of his clubs, trying to relax and think.

"Hey man, you got to stop being so hard to find. We got something serious to tell you." Jimmy was picked to do the talking and deliver the message because Alvin got along with him the best. Many had rumored that they were father and son.

"I know Stacy has been indicted. She'll be out on bond tomorrow. Everything is going to be taken care of." Alvin sipped on some Hennessy and smoked an expensive Cuban cigar. He didn't look up to recognize their presence, but he had looked. That meant he wanted to be alone.

Under any other circumstances, Jimmy would have walked back out and just left a note to be polite and waited for a phone call from Alvin. It was the practice for all. "We know that Stacy Dee has been indicted." He wanted to add that the whole city knew that Stacy Dee had been indicted. It wasn't a good time to be sarcastic. "We did something that we need to inform you about." Jimmy was moving real slow with what he had to put on the table.

This got Alvin's attention. He didn't utter a word. He looked toward Jimmy and made eye contact. His eyes and facial expression were telling Jimmy, *please don't say what he thought he was going to say*. Quadir and Tyrone looked the other way as if they were innocent parties. Alvin took note of how they were acting.

Jimmy had done all that he could to avoid the situation and made things as easy as possible. "We had to kidnap Stacy's mother and son." Jimmy looked back and forth between Alvin and his bodyguards. If they moved, he moved — just like that. His nine was holstered under his left arm with one in the chamber.

When Alvin banged the table and spilled his drink, he looked like he was about to jump out his wheelchair. The bodyguards didn't like to see their boss agitated like that. They unbuttoned their jackets and were ready to pull out their Tech-9s and nine millimeters.

Quadir and Jimmy were ready to hit the floor. Tyrone had his hand on his Uzi and was ready to get the first round of shots off.

"So, you motherfuckers went and disobeyed my orders." Alvin was ready to kill all of them on the spot. From experience, he knew that if he did, no one would make it out of there alive. If he could have just killed them without putting himself and his guards in jeopardy, he still wouldn't have done it — that might cause the death of his godson.

"We didn't exactly go against your orders." Quadir was prepared to say this moments after the last meeting. "You didn't order us not to do it."

Jimmy didn't want them to start arguing. There was too much tension and too much artillery in the room. "Ain't nothing gon' happen to Devon. I promise." This made Alvin look back at Jimmy. Quadir was still in the back and had his body poised to head for the door. His bulletproof vest, which he always wore under his clothes, wasn't enough to keep his life out of danger if his legs got shot up with an Uzi. "I got some of my own people at the spot and they got specific orders."

"So that's supposed to make me feel better?" When Alvin got mad, all he needed was some long, black, permed hair to look like Mr. Biggs.

"No, sir. That isn't supposed to make you feel better." Jimmy was always the perfect man to mediate. He hated being that at times because it put him right in the middle of gunplay, just like now. He was just a person that was just as peaceful as he could be, depending on the situation. "You are supposed to be mad, but we came to tell you before you found out from another source." Jimmy just wanted to get out of the room, knowing that emotions were going to cause a bloodbath before things could be resolved.

"So, was this your idea, Jimmy?" Alvin already knew the answer. He just wanted to make sure before he made a decision.

"No, sir. This wasn't my idea." Instead, he was mad as hell with Quadir and Tyrone for forcing him into this. He had no plans of letting that shit go.

"So, whose idea was it?" Alvin was calm.

Jimmy hoped that Quadir or Tyrone would speak up. Jimmy looked at the wall in an attempt to ignore the question.

"Jimmy, tell me whose idea this was." Alvin knew that Jimmy wasn't going to give up any information like that under any circumstances.

"I'm sorry, Alvin, but you know that I wasn't raised like that. And you know I love you like a father." Jimmy was twenty-five and had been partially raised by Alvin.

"Tell me whose idea it was," he ordered.

"Come on, Alvin. That doesn't matter. I'm promising you with my life that nothin' is going to happen to your godson." Jimmy stood up straight, like that was his last response.

"It was my idea," Quadir said. He was beginning to feel like Alvin was trying to chump him on the sly, which was true. It wasn't like it was a secret. He was the first one to mention kidnapping, and nobody else even said anything like that. Might as well put it out in the open.

"I know that. Now get the fuck out." Alvin thought a minute and waited until the other men had left. He said to his guards, "That nigga got to go."

There was nothing Alvin could do at the moment because his godson was being held hostage. He had made a decision that punishment had to be handed down because he felt that his position had been disrespected. If it took years to do, it would be done; this is what he told his bodyguards.

Chapter Five

When Stacy was brought to the interrogation room this time, the lights were turned on. "Bring her ass in here. I'm tired of playing games." Stacy recognized the voice. The tone was surprising. Even the female guard that was with her was surprised at the tone of voice.

Stacy knew that she really didn't want to hear anything that this cop had to say. She only wanted to hear from her lawyer and Alvin. There were two guys in the room this time, an older one and a younger one. She knew by the voice that the older one was the federal agent she had talked to before.

"So you are the notorious Stacy Dee. You sure don't look like much. My name is Special Agent Mark Matthews. I work for the Drug Enforcement Administration. This is my assistant, Special Agent Casey." He was acting like he had never laid eyes on her.

For over fifteen years, Mark Matthews had been trying to put The Untouchables under the jail. It all started when he was a detective for the Philadelphia police department. The Untouchables were the only group that he hadn't been able to lock up. His only reason for working for the DEA was to have the power of the federal government behind him. Every time that Matthews had a member of The Untouchables about to go to jail, something happened - the witness disappeared, the evidence disappeared the criminal was murdered, the rat was murdered, the rat's family was murdered or something went wrong. He almost arrested the leader one time. Instead, Matthews ended up in a shootout. Two of his police officers were murdered at the scene. They were supposed to have been ambushing a drug deal. Instead the drug dealers were waiting to ambush them and kill them. Parties from both sides were wounded and hospitalized. The defendants that were arrested and taken to the hospital for gunshot wounds all mysteriously died from different things the next day, so there was never a chance to interview them. Matthews was blamed for the deaths of his officers and of the prisoners because he jumped on a hunch that couldn't be considered reliable.

As a result, Matthews became obsessed with The Untouchables and with cleaning up his name, but he couldn't do it unless he was a cop. He didn't even know who he was chasing. But he knew they existed, just like the rest of the city knew they existed. The lead of his life was given to him a few weeks ago.

Stacy thought to herself, what part of the game is this? "So, the indictment got served and you act like we have never met. It isn't like you cheated on your wife."

Matthews laughed. "Read her the charges and let her know her rights." Matthews had come to the point that breaking the rules and the law was only a means to an end, as long as he didn't get caught. He loved how the feds operated, especially in comparison to the state. All the men on his team, including the Assistant U.S. Attorney, were from places that were far from Philadelphia. He was taking no chances on corruption getting in the way like it had done in the past.

When Casey was finished reading the indictment — it took about ten minutes — he laid it on the table in front of Stacy. It was thirty pages thick with twenty-five charges, ranging from drugs, murders, guns, conspiracy and racketeering. Other than the names of murder victims, her name was the only one on the indictment. If it sounded good, they put it in the indictment.

While Stacy was listening to the charges, she was thinking to herself that much of the stuff she was being charged with she didn't know about or it happened before her time. Is it really true that these people are trying to do me like this? Do these people think that I'm just going to bow down to this bullshit? She was just looking for that weak link or something that led to the rat.

"I heard your record," Matthews said with a snicker in his voice. "It's called 'I'm Bangin' 'Em'. Well, I'm about to start bangin' you. When you go to trial, we are going to play it for the jury." Matthews was trying to make Stacy mad and scared at the same time. "We know that you aren't responsible for most of this stuff in this indictment. We also know that you are going to get five life sentences. Three for the murders, one for the drugs and one for the guns." He had been pacing back and forth; suddenly, he got right in her face. "Little girl, do you think that you can do five life sentences?" He laughed and straightened back up. "Hell, you could beat one of the life sentences and still never get yourself out of jail."

Stacy hadn't thought about getting five life sentences. She just couldn't discount it because Jalissa had verified many of the things that Matthews had already said. There was nothing that she could think to say. Grabbing Matthews' gun and shooting him was a thought, but that would be a murder in front of the most reliable witnesses: cops. She would have to murder all of them — then hope to get out of the police station. If she got away, she would still be on the run and not be able to see her son. A real no-win situation. She just gritted her teeth and kept her mouth shut and tried to conceal her fear by maintaining eye contact.

"The Untouchables don't care about you, girl." Matthews thought he had her. It was time to push her closer to the edge. "You are going to have to watch your son grow up from prison, just like your father watched you. In fact, your father is going to be in the superseding indictment." He could see her pretty, dark brown skin turning reddish. He didn't know if it was because she was scared, mad or both. "You are going to do all of this time for a bunch of men that have no respect for you. They kidnapped your son and mother today."

"You are a motherfuckin' liar!" Stacy couldn't help it. "Nobody would ever touch my son! They know better!"

"If you're not smart enough to believe me, then you're probably not smart enough to help yourself. I'm tired of talking to this bitch." Matthews grabbed his jacket and stormed out of the room.

"He has a problem with his temper," Casey said in a relaxed tone to take over the case. "We keep telling him to stop drinking. I'm not going to let him hurt you."

Stacy welcomed the nice tone of his voice. She couldn't exactly concentrate because she wanted to know if her son and mother had been really kidnapped. It was something that she just couldn't take for granted.

Casey sat on the edge of the table. He started talking again when Stacy made eye contact with him. "I heard your song a few times. I think it sounded really great. If I could rap, I'd be trying to outsell Eminem." He had hit the button; Stacy smiled when she heard this. "It's going to hurt me to see you lose your chance at selling millions of records because of a few life sentences." Her smile went away.

It was time to go deeper. Casey was inside her head now. "It's true that The Untouchables have your son." He saw Stacy grit her teeth. "But, there is something that we can do about it. You don't deserve to be in prison, especially for some shit that you didn't do. Look at that pretty face and that pretty figure." He tried to get her to smile again.

"Don't fucking lie to me. Do they really have my son?" Stacy asked heated.

"Yes, they do." Casey shook his head like he really didn't want to tell her the bad news. He was now sitting on the table; any closer and and they would have been touching.

"Don't lie to me!" There was anguish in her voice that could only come from the love for a child. Stacy started to think that

that was why she couldn't get in contact with Al. Would Al kidnap his godson and threaten to kill him? There hadn't been any threats yet, but that was the usual thing to happen after a kidnapping.

Casey just nodded, frowned and fixed his eyes and face to look sad.

Paranoia started to slip in. "They're turning against me, and I haven't even been in jail but a week and a half," Stacy blurted.

"Yeah, that's what they're known for."

Stacy hung her head. Shit was gettin' real thick. Maybe it would have been better to stay in limbo. It was hard for her to think. She knew The Untouchables were capable of kidnapping to keep people quiet — she'd participated in a few, but nothing like this ever happened to anyone in the top of the organization. She didn't want to discount it. *Maybe they were convinced to turn against her.* All kinds of crazy thoughts were going through her head. It was all happening too fast for her to think straight.

"I care about you, Stacy. You got to help yourself." Casey could see that she was having a weak moment. That's exactly what he wanted to take advantage of.

The words were soothing. For a few minutes Stacy forgot that she was talking to a police officer. "What am I supposed to do? They have my son."

"We'll get your son back and protect you both." It was happening easier than he thought. Casey sensed that she was almost there.

"What about my mother?"

"Her also. We know you're a family."

"What am I supposed to do?"

"Just tell us everything, like they would do to you." Casey

drove at her with intense emotion. He could see that she was getting and closer to the edge. "Do you think they'd go to jail for you?"

Stacy was about to overload. Being on her period didn't help matters. All she could think about was her son. She would do anything to save him. Her internal dilemma was more intense than she ever thought imaginable. What would she really do if they really had her son? It would be like a slap in the face. Stacy had proven her loyalty to The Untouchables over and over. No matter; revenge is something she had to handle later.

"I can't help you. I'm not a rat."

Casey was surprised at response. "When you get the phone in your hand, you'll find out that they really have your son." He walked out of the room. Enough damage had been done, for now.

Just as soon as Stacy was back on the tier and out of the handcuffs, she was on the prison phone. "Lisa, please tell me it isn't true." There was more bass in her voice than usual.

"Tell you what?" Lisa thought that her partner was really slipping.

"The Feds say that my mother and son have been kidnapped by The Untouchables."

Lisa laughed. It didn't sound like something Alvin would order. She knew that Alvin loved Stacy like a daughter. "Get the fuck out of here."

This brought some relief to Stacy. "Well, have you seen them?"

"When I went by there, they weren't there and the car wasn't there. I figure they just went shopping or something." Part of Lisa's job was to go by the house every day to see that they were OK.

"Are you sure, girl?"

"Yes, I'm sure."

"Bye, bitch." Click.

Stacy wasn't satisfied with the answer. She went back to her cell to use the cell phone. She needed to talk to Alvin, but Alvin still wasn't answering the phone. "Damn, damn, damn." She tried all of The Untouchables. They weren't answering their cell phones either. As usual, they wouldn't pick up for unidentified callers. They had a thing about talking to people from prison on the phone — it was a no-no — since prison phones were always tapped.

Out of frustration, Stacy threw the cell phone up against the wall. It broke into a lot of pieces.

* * * *

"Yes," Matthews hollered. "Touchdown! Twenty-eight points for us, none for The Untouchables." He was so excited that he could taste the convictions, and he hadn't even started to use all of his tools.

"What are you so happy about? She just threw down what was helping us get plenty of information." It was Casey's first federal case. He had been watching and listening to Stacy for almost eighteen hours a day. He was paying his rookie dues.

"She's about to give up the rest of her crew because she can't get in contact with them. She just dialed three numbers that she hadn't used before. She's getting frustrated about her son and her mother. What mother wouldn't rat to save them?"

Casey thought about it for a minute. He was all about having hard evidence. He was new at making thorough investigations; the Feds were all about making rats. "I see what you are saying. I think I get it. She should crack after she gets denied bail tomorrow."

"Yes, yes, yes!" Matthews hollered like a surge of energy had just gone through his body. "She's going to get denied bail tomorrow. I did the legal research myself to make sure she isn't going to make bail. Why do you think I had her hit with all those charges?" Matthews had mapped out a plan that included all possible alternatives to make sure The Untouchables didn't slip out of the noose.

"So, she's really going to be hurt when she doesn't make bail."

"Yes, yes, yes. If she's not ready to tell by then, she'll damn sure be close to it." They just shook their heads.

"So now we need to find out where the other numbers that she called go to."

"I'm willing to bet that they are pre-paid cell phones, which is all right. We'll just get the phone records for those phones and see what other numbers pop up. Sooner or later we'll get a lead that'll get us a solid address instead of a P.O. box." All of this was standard procedure. Being that his partner was a rookie, Matthews felt that he could train him and trust him with the plans that he had.

"So, the object is to find out where all the other Untouchables live at and hang out." Casey was catching on fast.

"Yes."

"What about her speedy trial rights? She'll need to go to trial in ninety days."

"That's a good question. Her lawyer is going to file so many pre-trial motions that the speedy trial clock is never going to run out. There are going to be hearings after hearings. The longer it takes, the longer she sits in that cell by herself. Soon, we are going to take her toys and make life as miserable as possible.

Casey was rather impressed. He could see it all happening. He was just nodding his head.

"If we pick up the rest of The Untouchables, we can really put major pressure on them. They'll all be separated. Then, we'll pick up all of their workers. By that time, half of them will want to tell."

"That's how easy it is in the Feds?" In Mississippi, where Casey started his career as a cop, the police weren't that sophisticated.

"Once they're all indicted and off the streets for a few months, all hell is going to break loose. We'll have witnesses coming out of the woodwork." Matthews talked faster than he could think. It was all blueprinted in his mind. "I've seen it happen a thousand times."

"Then what do you do?"

"I'll retire." The look on his face said that he meant it.

Triple Crown Publications presents

Chapter Six

Friday, April 25
"What is next on the docket?" Judge Hackle demanded.

"We have a bail hearing and a preliminary hearing for *United States v. Stacy Dee*," the bailiff responded.

Jalissa stepped up to the defendant's table and waited for her client to be brought from upstairs. Matthews and Casey were sitting at the prosecution's table. It was the second case on the docket.

"Girl, what the hell is wrong with you? You look like you didn't get a bit of sleep last night." Jalissa was hoping the judge wouldn't notice Stacy's puffy face and red eyes. Jalissa felt that it would be OK since the Judge didn't know what Stacy looked like on a normal day.

"Are we ready to proceed?" the Judge asked Jalissa and the prosecutor.

"The defense is ready."

"The prosecution is ready."

Magistrate Judge Hackle commenced reading the charges. The more she read, the more disgusted she looked and kept looking at Stacy Dee. It was a judge's natural inclination to see the defendant as guilty when a slew of charges were in an indictment, especially for one person. Many others in the courtroom were taking more interest in Stacy as the Judge was reading.

"How does the defense plead?"

"Not guilty." Lawyers often wondered why preliminary hearings existed. Few defendants pleaded guilty at this stage, and even fewer had their charges dismissed.

"Now that that has been taken care of, we can talk about bail. What does the prosecution have to say?"

"Your Honor, there is no possible way for you to grant the defendant bail." Robert Parker was fresh out of law school[TMD2] and was going as hard as he could to make a reputation for himself. Matthews had liked him right away. "According to 18 U.S.C. 3142(f) (2) (B), a defendant can't get bail because of being a threat to witnesses and society."

Jalissa shot him a sharp look.

Parker was loving it. "We have evidence that Stacy Dee, the accused, is trying to find the rat in her case in order to eliminate him or her."

Stacy Dee looked across the room and thought to herself that it wasn't possible for them to know that.

"Plus, the gang that she is in — The Untouchables — have a reputation for making witnesses and evidence disappear. In fact, her mother and son have been kidnapped by the rest of The Untouchables."

Stacy looked at Jalissa in a way that asked if she knew anything. "That's why I haven't gotten any sleep," Stacy whispered in Jalissa's ear.

"Does the defense have anything to say?"

"Yes, the defense has something to say," Jalissa stood. "Your Honor, my client is a part-time college student. She's about to get her Associate's Degree. Surely you can tell, by the look of her, that she isn't old enough to be as dangerous as they say. She's presumed innocent until proven guilty. The prosecutor has presented no evidence about my client being violent or being a member of The Untouchables." Jalissa was shooting around the issue well. "Nor has he presented any evidence about a kidnapping. This trial may take a long time; my client deserves to be able to complete her education. It's only fair under the Eighth Amendment."

"Does the prosecutor have anything to add?"

"Yes, we do. I have a transcript from a telephone conversation that Stacy Dee had with a friend, whom we believe is part of the gang. In the conversation, in unequivocal terms, she is stating how badly she wants to find the rat."

The bailiff took a copy to the judge and a copy to the defense.

"This young lady is part of The Untouchables. We can't disclose our sources at this time for fear of their lives. In *United States v. Dominquez*, 625 F, Supp. 701, certain defendants were denied bail because they tried to hire a hit man to kill a snitch. This situation with Stacy Dee is the same." He passed copies of the case to the Judge and to the defense.

The judge read the case before their eyes and made a decision. "Bail denied." She hit her gavel. "Next case."

Matthews had to use all his strength to keep from jumping up in the air and celebrating. He just smiled at Stacy.

"There was nothing I could do Stacy," Jalissa said in her ear. "Al told me that he's going to get you out and that your people are safe. He promised that nothing is going to happen to them. He told me this personally."

Stacy couldn't say a thing. Matthews had begun to sweat her. The female guard came to make her go back to her cell.

* * * *

The pressure from being denied bail, finding out that her son and mother had really been kidnapped and the thought of having to be locked up for months before trial — Stacy remembered what her lawyer said —facing life sentences and the feds pressing her to rat, put her straight to sleep when she hit her bunk.

It was eight-thirty at night when she woke up. Stacy had slept for almost eleven hours. She didn't want to believe that so much had happened in less than two weeks. If someone had told her the same story, Stacy wouldn't have believed them. Her people turning against her was the thing that hurt her the most. She was wrestling with the idea of Al turning against her. They had a long history together and a bond she thought would never be broken. Stacy was now feeling that she had to question all things. There was nothing that she could think of to do. She was beginning to feel like they had broken the rules and left her out to die and be eaten up by the wolves. She felt alone, deserted, betrayed, used and stomped on.

Matthews and Casey wanted to immediately pull her back into the interrogation room. They would have, if it weren't a blatant violation of the attorney-client privilege. There was no need to take that chance. Just monitoring Stacy and her phone calls for the weekend would be enough. Matthews went home at six o'clock but Casey was still on the job. He was expecting Stacy to make a few calls before the night was out.

At ten o'clock, the female guard, who had given her the cell phone, tapped on the door to get Stacy's attention. Stacy looked up; she figured that she was being taken to see the fed guys again. She had been expecting them ever since she woke. The female guard gestured for her to come to the door. It was the same female guard that had been escorting her around. When Stacy got to the door the guard slipped her a package and a note. Stacy briskly walked back to her bed.

Yo Stacy,

Get ready to go. There are two Glock nines in the package, with a holster. Put the black sweats on and be ready to go in fifteen minutes. Al told me to come get you. Don't cut on your lights, and be quiet.

Stacy smiled back at the guard and nodded her head.

The sudden noise alerted Casey. He put his headphones on. The only thing that he heard was Stacy walking and moving around in the cell. He looked out of the window to see if her light was on. He figured she was just pacing, like most people in a cell do. He decided to keep the headphones on anyway.

Stacy was ready to go, just like the female guard had instructed. She had to put on two pairs of socks to make her prison shoes more comfortable.

When the guard came back she knocked on the door to see if Stacy was ready. They smiled at each other. The female guard stuck her key in the door and unlocked it with a slight noise.

When Casey heard the noise he thought that it was rather strange. There was no reason for him to hear metal touching metal at this time of night. He tapped into the jail's video surveillance system. He couldn't believe that he saw two hooded figures running down the hallway where Stacy was being held. The figures were wearing black and carrying guns. He called the police station, which was right downstairs, to let them know that Stacy was making a break for it.

When the desk officer found them on his video, they had burst through the exit door that led to the roof. As soon as they got there, sirens went off and lights from everywhere came on.

"I hope you're a good runner," the woman commented to Stacy.

"Shit, as good as I feel, I could run as fast as a cheetah."

"In a few seconds, the grounds are going to be filled with cops, ready to kill. We have to get past the cops and meet Alvin at the gate."   "Let's do it. I can run fast and I can shoot anything that's moving." Stacy was a little scared but her adrenaline was up and she felt like she could do anything. Her freedom was on the line and getting to her son was the only thing on her mind. The women took off running and made it to out the building with ease. Stacy stuck her guns in her holsters and started running as fast as she could.

"Freeze! Police! I'll shoot," a voice hollered behind her.

The women started shooting while Stacy ducked for cover. The guard wasn't going to let Stacy get shot if it was the last thing she did. The bullets were just inches from Stacy. She could feel them when they were passing, but she knew that the girl wasn't trying to shoot her.

She didn't flinch one bit. Stacy never changed her pace and made it halfway across the yard with ease. She looked behind her as she ran to see if the guard was all right and tripped over a rock. When she landed, her ankle twisted from the impact because of the prison shoes. Taking his chance, a cop on the side of the building fired his gun at Stacy. With killer instinct Stacy rolled over to dodge the bullet and fired back, killing the guard instantly.

"Get up, Stacy! They're getting closer! I can't keep them off much longer!"

Stacy complied and fired bullets from both guns. Lights were shining everywhere and cops were coming from every direction. Stacy didn't think that she would make it out alive.

"Come on, Stacy, we're almost there!" As they approached the gate, a cop on the roof , unbeknownst to Stacy, had his rifle aimed at her head. The guard Stacy was with caught it though and let off a shot first and hit him. "Let's go. The last part is easy."

Stacy wondered what she was talking about. She didn't see anything. Suddenly a gray van appeared. The doors burst opened and five of The Untouchables sprang out, spraying bullets. Overjoyed, Stacy started letting off rounds as well. It was just like the old days. Shots rang from an AK-47 and the cops ducked. When Stacy hopped in the van and saw the wheelchair and smelled Al's cigar, she hollered, "Alvin, what are you doing here?" and hugged him like she hadn't seen him in years. "I knew you were coming to get me."

The bodyguards were closing the van and firing shots at the top of the building to keep the cops at bay. There were three guards firing shots. One was at the end of the alley; one was on the ground in front of the van, and one was in the driver's seat.

"Let's get the fuck out of here. Don't forget my man at the front of the alley. We're shooting to kill if there's a high-speed chase."

Once they were far enough from the scene and they knew that nobody was following them, they started to talk.

"Alexis, you just did a wonderful job," Alvin said to the woman. "Here's a million dollars in cash, like I promised you."

Alexis thanked him. "If you need me to do anything else, I might as well because I'm never coming back to Philadelphia."

"There just might be something we can do. I know who the rat is."

"You know who the rat is? Tell me," Stacy hollered.

"Just chill out. We got to get Devon and your mother back home before I tell who it is."

"OK," Stacy said. She liked that idea. She hollered as loud as she could, "Devon, here I come, baby!!!"

Triple Crown Publications presents

Chapter Seven

It had been a long night for Matthews and Casey. They knew that they had screwed up majorly. Over and over again, they had to explain to the Philadelphia Police Department what they were doing with Stacy. Now it was time to face the music with the DEA.

"Well, Matthews, once again you've fucked up because of The Untouchables, and you are late." Billy Spanks was a young redneck who was in charge of the DEA field office in the Philadelphia area. Whenever there was a mess, he was the one that did the clean up. He was known to be that proficient.

Matthews really didn't give a damn. If anybody had gotten close enough they would have instantly sensed that he had been drinking all night. He started as soon as he could get himself away from the police station. He was tired of hearing about the cop that had gotten shot on the roof. His master plan had blown up in his face.

Casey had arrived to the meeting on time and had been there for an hour, making small talk with Spanks. Because he was just a rookie and following orders, there was really no pressure on him. His worst feeling was how the situation was going to affect Matthews.

"Matthews, come over here and sit with me," Casey said to comfort him. He could tell that Matthews really wasn't himself.

Spanks just shook his head. "Did you really think that two men, alone, could bring down The Untouchables? I told you that you could investigate, not indict and arrest."

Matthews looked up at his boss, who was ten years his junior. His expression said that he really didn't want to be there, let alone answer any questions. "We only needed one more week. She was about to crack."

"Damn, you held her hostage for a week, then indicted her, arrested her and made sure that she didn't get bail. What were you going to do next?" Spanks laughed his patented laugh, which he knew irritated people.

Matthews really couldn't believe what he had just heard. "In that period of time, we got more information than anybody else had gotten in the past ten years."

"Matthews, it's one thing to break the rules and get a conviction. It's another to break the rules and not get a conviction." Spanks really wasn't mad. He wanted to get The Untouchables almost as bad as Matthews but he had to bitch because he was the boss.

"What the fuck can I say? Shit happens." Matthews wondered if he was going to get fired or what. He shrugged his shoulders and put his head down.

"You know that I must take you off this case." Spanks continued to grin, which made his cheeks turn fiery red.

"Yeah, I know, man." Matthews had expected as much. This reminded him about the ambush so many years ago.

Spanks had seen a few cops lose their spirit because of the one that got away. Matthews' case was, by far, the worst. He had never seen a cop try to do a two-man operation, out of a police station, without telling the local authorities. He was wondering if Matthews would do something really drastic if Spanks decided to take him not just off the case, but also away from the case.

"You know they are going to hold you solely responsible for the cop's death." The cop hadn't died yet; he was just in critical condition. Spanks was just pulling Matthews' chain because he could.

This was the part of the conversation that Matthews really didn't want to hear or talk about. All night he had thought about what would happen to himself if the cop died. "Yeah, man," was all that he could say while he hung his head.

Casey was scared that Matthews was going to have a full breakdown.

"Matthews, look at me." It was time to stop playing. "That was a state cop. Fuck him. He was not DEA. And he wasn't a Fed."

"Yeah, he wasn't DEA," Matthews said out of instinct; he sounded like he still had some life in him. He liked the tone change of Spanks' voice and the words that were coming out of his mouth.

"To tell you the truth, what you tried to pull off was some of the most devious DEA work that I've ever heard of."

Matthews and Casey didn't know what to think of this comment. They just nodded their heads.

"With what you two have done, we are going to be able to close this case in a matter of weeks."

Matthews and Casey looked at each other in astonishment.

"You two deserve medals. We are the DEA and we look out for our own, no matter what they do, unless they get caught breaking the law. So far you only have an escape on your hands, a kidnapping and a cop killing that you didn't do. You didn't shoot that cop and you don't own a jail." All of this was meant to boost their morale.

It was music to their ears.

"I'm giving you a squad of DEA men to catch The Untouchables. Bring 'em in, dead or alive. Finish this case as soon as possible. Do whatever you got to do. Somebody has got to stand trial for that cop. All agencies are going to be behind you. If you have to break a few arms, break a few arms. If you have to break a few legs, break a few legs."

"I can handle it sir," Matthews said as he jumped up and saluted Spanks. "I'm not going to let you down." What he had just heard was better than having the Playboy of the Year for the weekend, with ton of Viagra.

"How are you going to do that?" Casey asked. "I mean, get an indictment on a Saturday?"

"We are the DEA and the Federal Government. We do what we want to do." Spanks let out another one of his laughs.

* * * *

On the other side of town the announcement that The Untouchables had been indicted had just come through the radio. Jimmy jumped out of bed when he heard the news. His being indicted along with all the other members of The Untouchables got his attention. His greatest fear was that The Untouchables would be indicted by the feds. Jimmy figured that the only thing that he could do was to get all The Untouchables back together as a team. His first move was to call his people that were helping to hold Devon and his grandmother and tell them go to Plan B. He had to see Quadir before he tried to find Alvin. Alvin and Stacy had to be plotting on how to get her son and mother back before they got arrested. Jimmy's vows to The Untouchables and his wanting to set things straight with Stacy kept him from skipping town.

Quadir and Tyrone were exactly where he figured he would be, at the Fifth Street Projects—a place where police of any kind were unlikely to come, unless they came as an army.

They had been arguing for about an hour. "We can't take on

the federal government and Alvin at the same time." Jimmy tried to use logic with Quadir. Tyrone didn't say anything, which was expected.

Coldly, Quadir responded, "And there is no way that Alvin can take on all three of us and the federal government." Quadir loved the way things were going. He was planning on having his way and then some.

"What happened to together we stand, divided we fall?"

Quadir didn't appreciate it when someone threw his words back at him. Tyrone was still standing on the wall, waiting to see what would happen. Quadir turned to face Jimmy. "There is no way that we can be together as The Untouchables when one of us is ratting."

Jimmy knew where Quadir was going. There was no response that he could make until Stacy's name was mentioned. There was the possibility of Quadir giving her the benefit of the doubt because she had escaped.

Quadir decided to take advantage of Jimmy's silence. "We need to know for sure that that girl isn't snitching. We know for sure that none of us are snitching."

"Come on, man. The girl escaped and killed a cop. Besides, we have her son and mother. How is she going to testify on us while she' on the run? Man, be serious." Jimmy knew in his heart that Stacy wasn't snitching.

"So do you think that Alvin is ratting?" It was more of a statement that a question.

Jimmy almost couldn't believe that Quadir would say something like that about the man that had taught them everything about the game. "Come on, man. That was some cold shit that you just said—you wouldn't let Alvin hear you saying that." There was a slight chuckle in his voice and a smirk on his face. He wanted to break up the tension of the conversation and make Quadir realize that they were going in the wrong direction.

"I'm serious."

"Nah, you can't be serious." Jimmy changed his expression and looked over at Tyrone with a is-there-something-that-I-should-know look. Tyrone just shrugged shoulders.

"I'm dead serious." Quadir took a deep breath to let what he had just said sink in, and to see if Jimmy had anything else to say. "What reason is there that we can't question him? So what, he brought us into the game and trained us and treated us like his sons?" Jimmy could see that something had gotten into Quadir and was making him extra power hungry. "There are only five of us in this crew. Who knows the most about all of us in the city? My workers don't know your workers that well, and vice-versa."

"What the fuck have you been drinking?" Jimmy had raised his voice considerably to make Quadir snap out of what seemed like a trance. Jimmy was tempted to walk over and shake the shit out of him but in Quadir's spot, that would be considered disrespectful.

"Nah. What the fuck is wrong with you? He's going to do the three of us so that he and his queen can rule the city. It's funny how the day after she escapes—an escape that he orchestrated—we all got indicted, on a Saturday. We are about to go down for a cop we have never seen."

"Well, why didn't he just make her a rat along with him, so that he wouldn't have to break her out—if he broke her out?" Jimmy was thinking at a furious pace to find holes in Quadir's theory. This was an argument that he couldn't afford to lose.

Tyrone nodded his head as if to say, that was a good point. He didn't feel like Stacy was really a rat, and he didn't want to turn on Alvin. He looked toward Quadir to see what he had to say. If Quadir had been looking directly at him, Tyrone's expression would have been different.

"So you see it my way." A smile had come across Quadir's face. "He's supposed to be fooling us because he's making moves that a rat wouldn't make. Or he may just want to get her out of the country. We're talking about Alvin, the genius. He's the man that has people going into the police academies and has people all over the city ready to do whatever he asks."

Jimmy had to admit to himself that Quadir's game was tight. "We all know that Alvin is the last motherfucker in the world that's going to be a rat. That motherfucker has kept The Untouchables untouched for at least fifteen years that I know about." Jimmy didn't know all of the history of The Untouchables, just like everybody else.

Quadir knew that Jimmy was going to go there. "There are plenty of top-of-the line cats that turned into rats. Alpo Scarpo was a rat for twenty years. Guy Fisher's codefendant, Nicky Barnes."

"You can't make sense of him being a rat. The Feds probably don't even know for sure that Alvin is the head of The Untouchables. They might not know what he looks like. They may not even know his name. For what reason is there for Alvin to turn rat? None." It took a minute, but Jimmy came up with something that Quadir couldn't compete with.

"OK, Mr. Pretty-Boy-turned-Mr. Smarty, who the hell is the rat?" Quadir's look had changed and he was feeling slightly disrespected. He saw the situation as the best opportunity for him to get Alvin's spot. He just wished that he could convince Jimmy to be on his side.

"So you want to change shit up because you can't find the perfect thing to say? You need to stop that shit, especially at a time like this. The Untouchables must come together." Jimmy knew that he had won this argument.

"So you haven't heard what I've been saying." Quadir didn't feel like trying to be persuasive and diplomatic anymore.

"Quadir, this isn't the right time for you to get on a power trip. It's the Feds, not the state, that we're dealing with." They had no respect for the state. They knew that Alvin could make the state do whatever he liked.

"Let me break it down to you like this. I know that I'm not a rat. I know that Tyrone isn't a rat. I know that you are not a rat. That leaves them two." They were eye to eye from opposite sides of the room.

Jimmy felt like he was about to be dragged into something else that he didn't want to be involved in, like trying to kill Alvin. He was glad that he had set in motion the moves to set Stacy's son and mother free.

"Look here, Quadir, it ain't time to start a civil war. We need to meet with Alvin and Stacy." He was still being the ultimate mediator.

Quadir turned around and unzipped his army fatigue jacket and looked up at the ceiling. Tyrone thought about saying something. Jimmy made eye contact with Tyrone to urge him to say something but was unsure. The silence lasted for about two minutes. Quadir turned around and aimed his nine millimeter directly at Jimmy.

"Jimmy, I got to know something," he said in a voice that was just loud enough to be heard.

Jimmy started to think that maybe this wasn't the argument to win, after all. "Is it that serious?"

There was a look of disbelief on Tyrone's face.

"Are you with us or against us? I got to know," Quadir said in a low growl. His eyes were squinted and beads of sweat were forming on his forehead.

Jimmy knew better than to say anything to provoke him. There was no time or room for slipping. The only way that he saw that he could survive was to get the gun from Quadir. "Is it that serious Quadir? Is it that serious, Quadir?" he kept asking as he walked closer and closer with baby steps.

In any other situation, Quadir would have already pulled the trigger, several times. As cold-blooded and diabolical as he was, he couldn't just shoot a man that was like a brother to him. "Answer me. Are you with us or against us?"

The last thing Jimmy needed to do was answer the question. He knew Quadir was the type to interpret answers however he wanted them to mean, especially open-ended questions. "Is it that serious? Is this the time?" If he could get Quadir to answer, then he would be one step closer to having control of the situation. He was four feet away from the tip of the gun.

"If you ain't with us, I'm going to have to kill you," Quadir responded while stepping backwards. He just wanted Jimmy to say that he was with them. That would have been enough for the moment. It would be better to kill him later, after he had won the war with Alvin and taken the number one position.

"I can tell that you really don't want to kill me. Is it that serious, Quadir?"

Tyrone was frozen. He couldn't believe what was happening. They were all supposed to be like brothers. If there was something that he could have done, he wouldn't have been able to do it because he was paralyzed from the shock.

Quadir felt threatened by the statement. Repeating the question didn't help matters either. He didn't want to ask Jimmy again. He had to do something different, for the sake of not being the same. "Are you with us or against us?" His anger wouldn't let him think of anything else to say. His back had just touched the wall. There was no more backing up. He could have turned sideways but that would have been acting too much like a coward.

"It ain't that serious, Quadir." In two more steps the barrel of the gun would be touching Jimmy's chest.

"Are you with us or against us?" Sweat trickled down the side of Quadir, near his right eye.

Tyrone prayed that Quadir would put the gun down, or that something to happen to keep him from shooting Jimmy.

"It ain't that serious," Jimmy said as he was about to put his chest against the gun barrel. He just needed to press up against it for a second so that he could get into position.

Quadir had come to the conclusion that Jimmy's walking up on him like that was a challenge. That was his way of rationalizing killing him. "It's that serious," he said when he pulled the trigger twice. He knew, by instinct, that Jimmy was trying to grab the gun. That was something that he wasn't going to let happen.

"Damn, Quadir," Jimmy hollered as he fell back and reached for the gun. When Jimmy's body hit the floor, Quadir shot him two more times, in the head.

Tyrone just stood there with his mouth wide open, looking back and forth at Jimmy and Quadir. As soon as possible he needed to get himself a hit.

Chapter Eight

Miss Jacobs was surprised to see Stacy when she opened her back door. "Girl, what are you doing out there in the dark and cold? Get yourself in here," she said with an enthusiastic voice that only a middle-aged female could use.

Stacy smiled and was relieved for the moment. No matter where she went, there was a chance that the cops would be watching the spot. Going directly to her man's house was out of the question. She couldn't take that chance, though she didn't think that they knew about him. One never knows. Calling his house was also out the question, even with a throwaway cell phone.

"Thank you, Miss Jacobs."

"You just set yourself down in the living room and make yourself comfortable. I'm going to get you some hot tea and cookies."

"Thank you, Miss Jacobs." In Miss Jacobs' presence she always felt a little nervous. Those moments she wished that she could be like other females—just graduating from college and embarking on a new career. Being a rapper was OK, but it wasn't like being a professional businesswoman.

It only took five minutes before Ms. Jacobs came back. "So, Stacy, why haven't you called me? I've been worried sick about you." Miss Jacobs drew the living room curtains and looked down the street to see if there were any strange cars.

Guilt ran through Stacy. The last thing she wanted to do was disappoint her boyfriend's mother. "Miss Jacobs, I'm in a bad situation. I really didn't want to disappoint you."

"Well, I'm disappointed something badly."

Why did she have to say that and say it that way? "Please accept my apology and know that it'll never happen again." She didn't want Miss Jacobs to find out what she was really into.

"Well, I'm going to accept that for now," Miss Jacobs responded in a slightly dignified tone that was meant to be understanding, but was also meant to say, I'm not going to forget.

"Could you please call your son over here?" Stacy sounded like she was really scared to ask this question.

Miss Jacobs responded with a smile, "I already did. I didn't tell him that you were here. I just had to say that it was an emergency." Miss Jacobs tried to let Stacy know that she knew what was going on.

Stacy didn't know what to say. Miss Jacobs just sat there with an expectant look.

"You know Stacy, I've kept quiet over the years about your profession." Sitting quietly, Stacy continued to drink her tea. "But now I feel that I have to speak my piece. My son really cares for you and so do I, but the life you're leading is not going to get you anywhere. I've been listening to the radio and watching the news and the media is portraying you as some kind of common criminal. I don't see that when I look at you but if you keep it up, that is what will you will become."

"I'm so sorry, Miss Jacobs, that I got you involved in all of this. I never meant to disappoint you but I had to do what I had to do at the time. All of that is in the past, though. I'm changing my life for the better, for me and my son."

"Good. Now that's what I like to hear. You know, I've listened to a few of your songs."

"Really," Stacy asked, shocked.

"Yes, and I actually quite like them. I respect you for the things that you have been through, Stacy. Despite all you've been through, you've still stayed strong for you and your son."

"Thank you, Miss Jacobs."

"No, thank you."

* * * *

Stacy and Jesse had just finished making love for the second time. The first time was really making lust.

Jesse got up from the bed and went to his pants. As he was about to pick them up, he said, "Stacy, baby, get up."

"Get up for what?" This was a strange request—one that Stacy didn't feel like fulfilling; there were many things on her mind. It was also in her gangster instinct to ask questions.

Jesse reached in his pants pockets and removed something. "Just get up and come over here. I have something for you." He knew this would make her get up.

Stacy smiled at the thought of him giving her presents. It made her feel special and feminine. No comments or questions were necessary anymore. These were the kind of moments that made her feel that Jesse was worth her time and efforts. Whether he knew that he was making her feel special and like a worthy woman didn't matter to her. It just mattered that he made certain moves at certain times.

"OK, boo, are we just going to stand here naked?" Stacy smiled from ear to ear. Sweat still ran down her body. Some of hers, some of his. A few drops had gathered together and ran down between her breasts. She loved to walk around naked in front of Jesse, especially when her nipples were hard. That power was the only thing that she had liked about being a stripper.

Jesse took a step closer. Stacy's nipples touched the bottom of his chest. Their hips touched as well, as if they were about to start dancing. He grabbed her hips and pulled her closer.

"I have something really special for you."

Stacy could tell that Jesse had a jewel box in his left hand by the way that he held her. Her lips were puckered in a way to say that she was happy, content and attentive. Stacy let him know that she wanted more of this attention by kissing him. Stacy pulled herself closer to Jesse by running her hands up his back to his shoulders and hugging him.

"So what do you have for me," she seductively whispered in his ear. She already knew that it was a ring or a pair of earrings because of the size of the box.

"You know I love you, don't you," Jesse asked to lay the foundation.

"Yes, baby. I love you, too." Stacy had never seen him act this way. Whenever she heard him say that he loved her she never took it seriously, though she wanted to hear him say it over and over again. Her smile had waned a bit. She searched his eyes for the answer to what was up with him.

"I'm talking about, I really love you." They were still holding each other tight. Prince's "Adore" was playing on the radio.

"What is wrong with you? Why you actin' all scared?" Stacy really wasn't sure of what to say or ask. She knew for sure that Jesse was scared. He was throwing her off because he was acting so differently.

"Oh baby, there is absolutely nothin' wrong. I mean, absolutely nothin'." Jesse pushed her to sit on the bed so that he could get more comfortable. Stacy was still smiling to be pleasant, but she didn't like when people acted differently. When Jesse got down on one knee, she said to herself, I know he isn't.

Jesse looked up and down Stacy's nude body. His left hand was strategically placed behind her back so that she wouldn't see the box. When his eyes met hers their stares locked. He paused and searched his inner feelings to determine if he was really feeling what he had been feeling for the past week.

If he asks me what I think he's going to ask me, I don't know what I'm going to do. Stacy bit her bottom lip to keep from yelling at Jesse to hurry up.

Jesse removed his left hand from behind her to show Stacy the box. There was just enough moonlight coming through the window for her to make out that the box was small and covered with brown velvet. The creaky sound of the box opening made the moment so much more intense that she wanted to grab the box. She bit down a little harder to suppress her emotions and actions.

"Baby girl, after you were locked up for about a week, I started to realize how I really feel for you." His voice was soft and caring. He was still on his left knee with a look of seriousness and sincerity.

"Oh yeah," Stacy replied in a high-pitched, breathy tone. She bit back down on her lower lip.

"I already knew that I loved you. I just didn't know how deeply. I was missing you so much; I knew then and there that Stacy is the only woman for me."

Stacy couldn't believe that Jesse was saying this, acting like this and on bended knee while they were in the nude. She felt so good inside that she was speechless and could only nod her head. Nothing but a murmur could come out.

Jesse placed his right hand on her left and spread his fingers to cover it. "Stacy."

She just nodded her head.

"I want to devote my life to you. I want to spend the rest of my life with you—children and all."

She continued to nod her head. *Oooh, I can't believe this!*

"Stacy." Jesse turned the box around so that she could see the contents.

She closed her eyes and put her hands up to her face. "No, you didn't! It looks so beautiful. Oh Jesse, I love it."

He had pimped this moment like a real playa. The sixteen-carat diamond ring had set him back nearly $60,000, half of his life savings. There was no way he would dare half-step with Stacy. "Do you like it?" Jesse asked, just to hear her say it again.

"Do I like it," she responded with a I-can't-believe-you-asked-me tone. "I love it!" Stacy was scared to touch the ring. Now, she could just be satisfied with the ring, since she couldn't take her eyes off it. It felt so good to be blown away.

"Let me put it on you." Jesse plucked the ring out of its enclosure and grabbed Stacy's left hand. She pulled back from nervousness and fear. "It isn't going to hurt." He could feel her tension when he grabbed her hand again. He had never seen her act like this. He had to pull a little harder than he had anticipated because she was putting up a bit of resistance. Her nervousness was making him slightly nervous.

Stacy couldn't take her eyes off the ring. She had never anticipated that Jesse would do something like this, though she had hoped. The way the moonlight made the diamond sparkle had her almost hypnotized. She felt good but scared. Never before had she felt so special. As Jesse was about the slip the ring on her finger Stacy felt like the world had stopped turning.

With the ring just hanging over her fingernail, Jesse looked her in the eyes. He had to tilt her chin up to get her eyes to meet his. He had thought about this for days. As he prepared to slide the ring into her finger, he thought that this is what he wanted.

Staring in her eyes let him know for sure.

"Stacy." She was speechless and numb. As he finally slid the ring on her finger, he asked, "Stacy, would you marry me?"

Damn, he asked me! Instinctively, Stacy said, "Yes, I'll marry you," and kissed him on his lips. She knew that he loved her. Nothing had prepared her for what had just happened. They stood together and continued to kiss passionately. Without warning, Stacy broke away from him and ran to the window. Jesse grinned. He had did the damn thing. Stacy wanted to look at the ring closer without turning the lights on. The moonlight was enough.

"I love you," she said, attacking him.

Kissing his lips hungrily while he massaged her ass cheeks, Stacy moaned. Licking his ears and neck she made her way down. Taking his dick in her hand she wrapped her lips around his manhood and sucked. Running his fingers through her hair Jesse groaned. Stacy had missed the taste of him. Jesse was just how she liked him, good and hard.

"Baby, I can't take it no more. Get on top," Jessed begged, not wanting to cum yet. Taking her cue, Stacy eased her way down onto his thick, hard dick. Holding her waist Jessed guided Stacy's body up and down.

"Oooh you feel so good," Stacy moaned, pinching her nipples. Flipping her over onto her stomach Jesse eased his way back in and began hitting it from the back. Playing with her clit Stacy felt another orgasm coming along.

"Yes baby, yes! Right there!" she yelled as her legs began to shake.

"Right there?" Jesse said hitting it harder.

"Yes, right there! Don't stop!" Screaming and calling out his name they both came together in unison. Still not satisfied, Stacy attacked Jesse again and made passionate love to him, like they hadn't already had sex at all. She did to him whatever could be imagined, things that she had never done with him. With her heart, mind, soul and imagination she went all out. No shorts for her future husband.

Stacy woke up about an hour before Jesse did. Part of her was thinking that last night had to be a dream. Nah, it couldn't be a dream because the ring was still on my finger. She knew that they'd definitely made love because she could still smell it in the air and feel the great feeling of just being pleasantly sexed. With the present situation—cops chasing her and The Untouchables, and her son and mother being kidnapped—getting married just didn't fit in. She got out of bed so that she could think clearly. Putting on her clothes, she stood by the window and thought about the predicament she was in, but every time Jesse moved and touched her, her feelings of love and passion sparked up and got in the way.

When Jesse woke up he rolled over to find his future bride. He was surprised to find himself alone in bed. He jumped up to see if Stacy was in the same room. Her laugh let him know that she was still with him.

"Why are you laughing at me? And why do you have your clothes on? We have to make love one more time." He looked at her as if there were no way for her to deny him.

She was taking much enjoyment just watching him sleep. The way he woke up really touched her. It was the closest that she had seen him act jealous. "We have to have a serious talk, Jesse." With the way he was acting, there was no way for her to beat around the bush.

Jesse looked up at the ceiling, then around the room, as if she were joking. "What are you talking about? You are getting ready to be my wife and that is that." There was an unquestionable sternness in his voice.

When had Jesse ever talked this way, Stacy wondered. There was a new tone in his voice. It had taken her by surprise and caused her to recalculate her thoughts.

"So what are you going to do? The sun is coming up soon. We got to do it just for the road." He beckoned her to the bed.

Deep inside, Stacy wanted to go to him and lose herself in him. "We got to talk, baby." The purpose-driven part of her kept her on track.

Jesse laughed. "We can talk about our honeymoon and kids when you get over here, so I can get some more of that good pussy."

Stacy blushed. "This is serious, boo," she screamed to get his attention and remain respectful.

"Damn, so you gon' fuck up an entire date? If I did that, you'd be cursing me out." Jesse was intent on getting his way.

"Baby, how are we going to get married, with me on the run? What kind of life are we going to live?"

"I don't care. All I care about is that I love you and I want to marry you." He was sat at the edge of the bed and talked like he was possessed.

Stacy couldn't believe that Jesse was being so aggressive. "I don't think that you understand." The growl of his voice echoed in her head and turned her on.

"Baby, I'm a thinker." Jesse was now on his knees, leaning on her lap and in her face. "I know what the fuck is going on."

Stacy pushed him back and got out of the chair. "It doesn't sound like you know what's happening. How we gon' get married and have kids? I might end up dead or with a few life sentences." She stood over him and hollered so that he couldn't take control.

Jesse stood up as well and got eye to eye with her. "You don't understand. I'm plannin' to make sure that you don't die and don't go to jail. I got guns, too."

A look of surprise came across her face. "Yeah," is all that she could say.

"Yeah. When y'all strap, up I'm strappin' up also. Remember I was born in South Philly. Do you *understand*?"

Stacy just shook her head. "OK, you undercover gangster. If you really want to marry me, we got to make it through this. I ain't marrying you from the penitentiary. It's pimp or die."

"Yeah, it's pimp or die. Before that, it's you and I gettin' busy. Now, lets do it," he demanded.

Another one of her dreams had come true.

Chapter Nine

Sunday, August 27
During the day, Stacy, Alvin and the ex-cop and bodyguards were literally underground. Alvin owned a grocery store that had underground living quarters for ten people. The only people that knew about this place were his bodyguards, himself and the store manager. When it was time to eat, they just went to the store and got what they needed. Stacy was really impressed.

Alvin was doing his usual cigar smoking and sipping on Hennessy. Since his incarceration, he smoked two Cuban cigars and drank a fifth of Hennessy on a daily basis. "Stacy, I need to get you out of the country. Shit is getting ready to get real hectic. I don't want you around anymore."

That really got her attention. It made her put down her book— *M.T. Pimp*— that she had wanted to finish for the longest. "Alvin, this federal indictment thing hasn't made you change, has it?" She walked over to him to make sure that she heard every word and saw all of his emotional responses.

"No, baby girl, I haven't changed. The situation has changed," Alvin said before he started to cough in a manner that indicated a deep sickness.

Stacy patted him on his back. "For sure, you need to get to a doctor about that cough. It sounds like you are about to die."

She sat in his lap and hugged him like she had done since she had met him. He wheeled them over to the couch where she had been sitting and pushed her back onto it. "So, you don't want me to touch you now," Stacy said with disgust as she sat on the couch.

"We have to have a serious conversation. It's time for you to leave. I have no control over what may happen next, and I don't want you to get hurt."

His not wanting her to get hurt was understandable and something that Alvin said many times before. "So, you don't want me in the Untou—"

"I told you to never say those words unless you had to, unless you know there are no bugs around. You know who you are and what you are. And that isn't the situation. I want you to always be around me because we have that kind of love. The Feds are on your back and we have a rat to find. It was always easy to find the rat. It may be time to retire."

"*You forgot something.* My son and my mother." Stacy folded her arms across her chest.

"Oh yeah. They're at my mansion. Some of Jimmy's people brought them over there."

Stacy wasn't sure what to say. It wasn't like Alvin to hold back information. "When did all of this happen?"

"I found out last night while you were out. I've been thinking so much that I didn't want to tell you too early and cause you to run out and get caught by the Feds. I'm sure they're watching my mansion."

Stacy had to admit that she was ready to run to her son, just like she had been ready to go blast the other members of The Untouchables as soon as the escape was over. "Are my son and mother OK?"

Alvin started coughing when he tried to take a puff on his

cigar. "They're fine. I was told…they're still at the mansion. They'll be safe there."

"So why did they decide to let them go?" It didn't matter to her that the kidnapping was over. It mattered that it had happened. Something still had to be done. Forgiveness wasn't an option. Forgetting wasn't possible. Revenge was mandatory.

"I don't know. Jimmy probably got them out of there. He didn't seem like he was really with it from the start and he tried his best to smooth the situation over. It was his people that delivered them." Alvin wondered privately why he hadn't been able to make contact with Jimmy.

"Well, I hate to say this, and be salty at a time like this, but Quadir and Tyrone got to pay for disrespectin' me and my peeps." Stacy's tone indicated that there was no way for her to change her mind.

Alvin pinched the bridge of his nose. He was hesitant to speak because it was a tense situation. There had been beefs, strife and problems with members, but never any disrespect— and definitely not a kidnapping.

"I understand how you feel. I'm not going to try to change your mind. I'd feel the same way. What good is it to get your revenge, then to do a few life sentences? We just have to go overseas to a place that won't extradite us, and come back when we get ready. I want to get them also." Giving Stacy an order would have probably made her mad enough to buck.

"Damn, Alvin! I ain't never heard you talk like this." Stacy wondered if her man and Alvin had exchanged souls and hearts. "There has got to be something really wrong, and wrong with you. You are supposed to be saying, 'Let's get this or that motherfucker and find out who the hell is ratting'."

"You ain't listening to me. You can leave with your son, mother and your fiancé. I saw the engagement ring. It's getting ready to get really bloody and the Feds are waiting on every corner for us to show our faces."

"I love you for what you are saying. I love you like my man and my father. I'm still a bitch. Not the kind of bitch that runs, but that gangsta bitch of all bitches. Before I leave this city, somebody is going to regret putting their hands on my son," Stacy raged as Alvin was just shook his head. There was nothing he could say. "We goin' in blazin'. Fuck them bitches."

"Damn, girl. Think about your son and your mother and your future husband. You can walk away and come back if you want to."

"That ain't good enough. *I want them now*. They should have respected my gangsta." Stacy remembered how badly they had treated her when she was just a soldier and a worker.

"Damn, girl." Alvin just shook his head again and questioned how they could have ever doubted her. "I guess there is just plain gangsta in your blood. We go to do what we got to do."

* * * *

"Don't cut the light on," Stacy said to Lisa in a tone that made the statement sound like an order.

Lisa had locked her apartment door and was about to turn on the dining room light. She had just come from the club at four in the morning. "Damn, bitch! It's about time that I heard from you," Lisa responded in an excited tone. She walked toward the chair from which she heard Stacy's voice.

Clickety clack; it sounded as if Stacy were putting one in the chamber of her gun. *Swoosh. Swoosh. Clang. Clang.* Lisa's glass living room table broke into three pieces.

Lisa stopped mid-motion. "What the fuck you do that for?" Her buzz from smoking weed, drinking and partying disappeared.

"Sit down on the couch, Lisa. We got to talk."

Lisa was more surprised than scared. Stacy had taught her to not show any fear, even when her heart was pumping fast. Lisa was hesitant to move because of her disbelief. Maybe Stacy was playing a joke.

"I'm dead serious. Nobody will know that I killed you. This isn't a joke. *Sit down*!"

The iciness of Stacy's voice let Lisa know that she was ready to kill her. They knew each other that well. "Oh, OK. Whatever you want." There was a slight tremor in Lisa's voice.

"That's it. I'd hate to kill you for no reason at all. I just want to ask you a few questions." Lisa sat on the couch. "Now throw your pocketbook in the middle of the floor." Stacy knew that Lisa kept a .380 in her purse. Lisa threw her purse just far enough for it to land on the other side of the broken glass.

"Sit farther back on the couch." Stacy wasn't taking any chances. She wanted Lisa's back to be resting against the back of the couch. Alvin taught her to not take risks, even when you thought someone was unarmed. One could never tell.

"Why the fuck are you trippin'?" At any minute, Lisa figured Stacy was going to start laughing and tell her that she was playing a joke.

"Don't make me nervous, Lisa. This is serious as a motherfucker. Just lean back on the sofa and get comfortable." The only thing that Stacy could see in the dark was Lisa's figure. She wanted to turn on a light. "That's it. Now I can relax." She said that to make Lisa relax. Stacy turned on the lamp that was next to her chair. She wanted to see all of Lisa's facial expressions.

Damn girl, you don't look like you just broke out the county jail, Lisa thought to herself when she saw the glow on Stacy's face. "So, you escaped from the jail so you could come kill me," Lisa said with sarcasm.

"No." Stacy ignored both the question and the tone of voice.

She answered 'no' to be polite. "I need to know where you were at the day before my indictment came down."

"You think that I'm a rat," Lisa hollered and jumped to her feet.

Stacy leaned back in the chair and pointed the gun directly at her.

"No. I have a few more questions."

"Damn, bitch! I ain't the rat." Lisa's anger made her sweat.

"Tell me about the new cell phone that you suddenly decided to pick up."

"Dang. This cat came to the set and was selling them real cheap. I got one for me and one for you."

"We got a cell phone connect? What the fuck is you now, the boss?" Cell phone purchases were a decision that only Stacy was supposed to make.

"The shit was cheap. Real cheap. They all have a thousand minutes a piece for just $50. I thought you'd be proud of me." Lisa's leg started shaking because of the look that Stacy gave her. "I'm sorry, bitch. I thought it was a good move," she said to cover up her fear but her tone gave her away.

Stacy wondered if she should press her partner some more or should she let it go at that. There wasn't enough of anything to infer that she was a rat. "So why the fuck they didn't indict your ass?" She figured that the Feds had to know by now that Lisa was her main girl. For sure, the rat knew this.

"How the fuck am I supposed to know that? I'm not one of them." Lisa though that if she was going to get shot, she might as well go out like a soldier, so she put some bass in her voice. Before she had spoken like she had to go to the bathroom.

Stacy began to feel like she was dead wrong. "If it turns out that you are a rat, I have people that are going to do your entire family." It was something that she really didn't want to say, but had to, though it was a bluff.

"I understand."

"You know that you may get indicted and arrested, and may face a life sentence." If the response wasn't acceptable, Stacy was going to put bullets in her forehead and at the base of her skull, just as Alvin had taught her.

"I'm true to the game and it's going to be pimp or die. I can't turn on you. You helped me get all that I got."

Stacy stood up. "Come give me a long hug, girl. I'm sorry. I'll pay for the table." They hugged each other. "I'm sorry, bitch. It was business. I couldn't have hurt you."

They let each other go. "Shit, bitch. You sure had me fooled. You had me scared to death."

"Look, girl!" Stacy put her hand under the lamplight. "Jesse and I have plans to get married."

"Damn, bitch! All the good shit happens for you." A wave of jealousy went through her. If Stacy had been looking at her friend's face, she would have seen it as clear as a newspaper headline.

* * * *

"Did you have to kill Jimmy?" Tyrone had stayed away from the Fifth Street Projects since Jimmy's murder. There was only so much cocaine, heroin and gambling that he could do before his thoughts and feelings led him back to Quadir.

Quadir had been waiting and was ready to go to the next phase of his plan. "Right now, you don't understand. But a few years from now, you will." Carrying Tyrone was part of his plan. He knew that it was a matter of time before he had the rest of Tyrone's soldiers and property.

"He was our brother." The Untouchables weren't going to be the same. He didn't want to see Quadir and Alvin going at each other. If they ended up killing each other, it wouldn't surprise him. It was the last thing that he wanted.

"I'm hurting, too, because Jimmy was a true general in every sense of the word, and a diplomat. I couldn't convince him. He wouldn't back down. He even turned Stacy's son and mother loose." Quadir's tone was inviting and slow, like he was talking to a child. Before the meeting was over, he was planning to make Tyrone take a bath. He was the only one that got to see Tyrone in this condition.

Tyrone dropped to his knees. "Did you have to kill him? Shit ain't gon' be the same." He didn't care about Stacy's son and mother.

"Listen. The Untouchables are still going to exist. One of them is a rat. We get to the rat and the Feds won't have a case." Quadir was up in Tyrone's face. He pressed his fingers and thumb against a pressure point in Tyrone's wrist for emphasis.

"I don't know, man. How the fuck are you going to get at Alvin? That motherfucker is really untouchable."

Quadir stood up. A frown came across his face. "He's about to be touched. I'm going to touch him."

"Damn, Quadir! Don't you know how much artillery he has?" Shaking his head, Tyrone stood and grabbed Quadir by the shoulders. "How the fuck are you going to get around those crazy bodyguards?"

"What makes you think that I won't ice his bodyguards?"

"What makes you think that you are going to be able to catch them slippin'?" Tyrone wished he could find a way to resolve the matter without there being a war. He really didn't want Quadir to be the number one.

"I've got a project's worth of killers that are ready to move on my word. We'll get to them if they're in the city."

There was no need to argue that point—Quadir had Philadelphia's biggest army. Plus, knowing Stacy and Alvin, they were probably thinking the same thing and mad about the kidnapping and ready to go to war. Tyrone didn't want a war because he wasn't going to benefit. His position in The Untouchables was going to be the same if he could stop his bad habits. In fact, he knew that his bad habits were going to get him put out of The Untouchables, and probably killed. Quadir was his only hope for hanging on.

"I guess we are going to war," Tyrone said as he ran to the trashcan.

He grunted as his body heaved and pushed up what little there was in his stomach, mainly acid and bile. He hadn't eaten in days. Quadir privately thought to that in less than three months, it would be all over for Tyrone. Because he was still somewhat useful, it wasn't time to end his life even though he was an embarrassment to The Untouchables.

"You need to get yourself straight. Soon it's going to be time for The New Untouchables to take over. You are going to be the number two man." That was a dream that Quadir sold to Tyrone to keep him useful until it was time to kill him.

"Yeah, man. If we get rid of them, then there won't be a rat and the feds won't be able to fuck with us." Being number two sounded pretty good to Tyrone. He wasn't planning to argue with Quadir, for fear that he would end up like Jimmy.

"To be the number two, you got to do better than you are doing." Lyrics to keep the press on and to keep Tyrone under control were what Quadir was spittin'.

"Yeah, man. It's just a matter of time. I'll be able to kick these monkeys when this thing is over." Tyrone felt like he might puke again. If anything came up, he planned on holding it in his mouth.

"I'm going to make The New Untouchables truly invincible and untouchable. With you by my side, there will be no stopping us. We'll go on and take over the entire city, like we should have done years ago." Alvin knew that greed could easily destroy an organization. His philosophy was there's no need to expand when you are making more money than you should be spending and keeping peace with the other hustlers. He understood more money, more problems. Quadir disagreed.

"Damn, if we do that, we'll be making more money than we'll be able to count. We're already making a mint now." Tyrone thought that he could now bet $50,000 on every sporting event so that he could get back to even.

"Yeah. We won't have to split shit five ways. It'll just be me and you. I'll be sixty, you'll be forty." Quadir liked the idea of fattening the pig before the slaughter—then he wouldn't have to share with anyone.

"That sounds like a great plan. I'm in all the way. When do we kill Alvin and Stacy?" Greed had set in. Plus, Tyrone was tired of Quadir taking advantage of his bad habits. With enough money, he figured, he'd be able to make it without having to borrow any money.

"That's all Jimmy had to do: go along with the plan." This was Quadir's way of telling Tyrone that he could be next. His sinister laugh should have been enough to alarm Tyrone.

There were other matters pressing Tyrone for him to really notice what was going on. "Yo, man, I need $25,000 to hold me until this matter is over."

Quadir could read him like a book. "How the hell are you going to pay me back? We got a drought and a civil war about to go down—not to mention, the Feds on our backs."

"You just told me how great things are going to be when we take over. You can wait until then, can't you?"

"Listen. I love you like a brother, except when it comes to my money."

"OK, man, what the fuck do you want?"

"Well, you know that house that you have over on Roosevelt Blvd? Let me get that for $50,000."

"That's a $200,000 house!"

"$50,000 is worth that to you at the moment. We ain't got no drugs and no cash flow right now. So what are you going to do?" Quadir loved moments like this.

"You are just going to start taking my shit instead of taking liens, like you have been doing?"

"OK, then, a lien is good." This was all Quadir wanted from the start.

<u>Chapter Ten</u>

Monday, August 28
Since Friday, an all points bulletin had been put out on Stacy and the cop that had helped her. This was mostly the state's work. The Untouchables had been added to the bulletin.

"People, listen up," Spanks said getting everyone's attention. A special task force had been put together over the weekend. Five members of the task force were from the state but mainly it was a federal thing and a federal beef. There had never been an escape from the FDC. "We are going to catch all of The Untouchables before it's all over. It brings me pleasure to say that it's the end of The Untouchables."

Matthews thought that he should be the one making the speech and leading the posse. If it weren't for him, the ball wouldn't be rolling in the direction that it was.

"We believe there's a war going on between members of The Untouchables. Some of them kidnapped Stacy's son and mother. We know for sure that the kidnapping took place. We heard about it from our confidential source and over Stacy's cell phone. As of yesterday, though, the son and the mother have been rescued or something. They're at Alvin's mansion in Chestnut Hill. We've had it under surveillance since Saturday."

"Excuse me." Matthews stood up. "Did you say that Stacy's son and mother were rescued from the kidnappers?"

Spanks didn't welcome this interruption. "We have pictures of them at Alvin's mansion."

"Maybe Alvin is holding them hostage," Matthews countered. He wanted to make it known that he knew the most about the case.

"According to our confidential informant, Alvin was the one that pulled off the escape from the inside." Spanks was trying to make Matthews upset.

"So does that mean that Alvin didn't have anything to do with it?" He already knew the answer because he was in constant contact with the confidential informant.

"OK, smart ass. The C.I. said that he helped with the kidnapping and that Jimmy had his people turn them loose." Spanks' neck turned red, a sure indicator that he was angry.

"OK. That makes sense." Matthews took his seat.

"People, we have some easy convictions because we have a C.I. that knows plenty about The Untouchables. We also have plenty of evidence to corroborate the testimony." For years Spanks kept hearing that people were scared to testify against The Untouchables. At times he wondered if The Untouchables really existed. Hearing about them always made him mad, especially because he couldn't figure out who they were, or if they really existed.

Spanks continued. "Alvin is the man we want. We don't want him dead or hurt." He had been keeping up with Alvin for a long time because it was rumored that he was the leader of The Untouchables. He couldn't find anything to connect him to any criminal activity but that feeling in his gut caused him to keep watching. "We figure that Alvin and Stacy are together and plotting to find the C.I.'s identity. Or, they might try to leave the country. As long as we keep an eye on the son and mother, at least Stacy can't get away. She loves that little boy. Where the son goes, we go—even if it's out of the country."

"So what are we going to do, great leader?" Matthews spat. Spanks being in charge was just as bad as being off the case. He knew that Spanks was planning to take all of the credit for bringing down The Untouchables.

"We are going after Quadir, Jimmy and Tyrone. Quadir is going to be the easiest to get. He thinks that he's real safe in the Fifth Street Projects, with all those gun-happy kids around him."

Matthews wanted to holler something about when they were going in. He knew that it was going to be tough as hell to get Quadir off the top floor of the Fifth Street Projects. It was rather impossible without getting a bunch of officers killed.

"We'll have the element of surprise on our side. Quadir doesn't know that we'll be able to get through his young thugs."

Many of the cops in the room started to look at each other. The Fifth Street Projects were known as a no-man's land. When the cops went to arrest somebody, they went twenty deep, with M-16s and AK-47s, like they were on a military operation. Going after the leader of the projects was a different story. A shootout was unavoidable. They knew the kids in Fifth Street were just waiting for an opportunity to shoot at some police officers.

"We aren't going in there tonight." Spanks had expected a negative reaction from his men and he couldn't blame them. Everybody knew that Quadir had many of those kids thinking that he was life itself. "We have a plan that includes the National Guard. We are going to practice before we go in, which will be less than three days."

Matthews hoped that the plan would blow up in Spanks' face. Regardless, he had to get in a comment. "What about Jimmy and Tyrone?"

"We are going to pick them up on site. They'll show their faces before it's over. This meeting is adjourned. Matthews, I need to speak with you."

Matthews was more than glad to wait up. No sooner than the other officers were out of earshot, Matthews set the tone. "I don't like what you are doing."

"I don't like the fuck what you just did!" Spanks made sure he was speaking louder than Matthews.

"You are not going to steal the credit for my case!"

"This shit is wrapped up and there is nothing that you can do. Get the fuck out of my office. The Untouchables are mine."

* * * *

Stacy had been up for about an hour. She was glad to see Alvin finally come in the living room. "It's time that we make that move on Quadir. He's still hanging in his perch like a fool." She munched on a breakfast bar. Her deep-set eyes looked well rested.

Alvin had been thinking the same thing. "So what happened with you and Lisa?"

"I don't think that she's the rat. I really can't see her knowing enough to make a case against anybody but me."

"So you don't think that she's the leak?"

"You never know, but nah. She was really scared when she saw that I had a gun on her. She thought that I was playing a joke and acted like I was disrespecting her. I would have really wondered if she hadn't acted disrespected."

"Well, let's see if you think it's who I think it is."

"Shit." Stacy laughed. "It's got to be Quadir. He wants your spot badder than a motherfucker wanna fuck Halle Berry." She was glad that Alvin asked.

"Yeah, I'm thinking on the same lines. But who's going to respect him in that position as a rat?"

Stacy shook her head. "You got a point there. Who the hell is going to go after him, even as a rat? He'll just tell his followers something slick to make them accept it."

"You got a point. Them youngsters worship the ground that he walks on. But I don't think that it's him." Alvin lit up a cigar.

"So who do you think it is? And why you lighting up that cigar? You'll be coughing in a minute."

Just as she said it, it happened. She went over to him and patted him on his back. "I think it's Tyrone," Alvin sputtered.

"Nah. Why would he go out like that?" Stacy had never thought that Tyrone could be the one—not the most violent cat in the crew.

"He's about to go broke and lose his position. He knows he'll have to be put out—all the way out. So what does he have to lose except his pride? He'll be a legend, like the other big time snitches."

Stacy really didn't know what to say. She massaged Alvin's shoulders and neck. "Damn, you got a point. He owes me some money, about $50,000. It's been over a year. I still ain't feeling him doing that, nor Jimmy."

"Jimmy tried to clear things up. At first he agreed to the kidnapping." A surprised look crossed Stacy's face. "He changed his mind when I reminded him that he would feel disrespected if it happened to him. I know that boy better than he knows himself. He was always trying to be peaceful when possible." Alvin was wishing that he could get Jimmy to the hideout so they could talk.

"Well, I can feel what you are saying about Tyrone." Stacy really didn't, though. It was about the kidnapping. "We can get Quadir and Tyrone on the same night. I just want to do Quadir myself. I know it was his idea to fuck with my peeps."

There was no need to tell her that she was right. "Do you

want to get him because he's a rat, or because he kidnapped your peeps?"

Stacy wanted to say both, so she took a few seconds to answer. Alvin's tone of voice made her feel like she had to be cautious about her answer. "Well, he disrespected me."

"So what do we do after all of that?"

Stacy wondered where Alvin was leading her. "I'll be ready to leave the country, if that's what you want to do." She also figured that there was no need to leave if Quadir was the rat.

"You know you ain't gonna want to leave the country. You won't be able to do your rap thing like you want to."

Stacy sucked her teeth. "OK, Alvin. You got me. Where are you trying to drive me to? I know you, Alvin."

"I'm going to do something for you, then you are going to do something for me."

"Go ahead." She stopped massaging him.

"We are going to go get Quadir and give him what he deserves."

"You are going to do that for me?"

"Yes, I'm going to do that for you."

"Stop lying, Alvin. You know that you want to do Quadir just as bad as I do."

"But I'm going to do it for you. I was ready to leave the country when we heisted you. We would have, if your son and mother hadn't been kidnapped."

"Whatever you say."

"Do we have a deal?"

"One thing. Can Jesse come with us when we get Quadir?"

"Your man, the accountant. What brung this up?"

"He said that he wants to roll when we roll."

"I can't do that. He ain't got no training. This is going to be real delicate."

"That'll be a nice favor to me."

"I just need you to owe me one big one."

"Alvin, I need to see what he's made of before I decide to marry him."

"We can't take that risk."

"We'll just let him ride in the car. Let him be a driver."

"His pride might get in the way."

This made sense to her. "So what will I owe you?"

"I'll let you know, I'll let you know real soon."

Chapter Eleven

Wednesday, August 30

"Our time has come," Quadir hollered over his crowd of followers. He was standing on four stacked milk crates. There were about one hundred cats in the basement of the Fifth Street Projects. Quadir had waited for the perfect time to make this speech. Tyrone stood to the side. The crowd had been waiting for almost an hour for Quadir to come down from his perch on the tenth floor. "That's right, Fifth Street is about to take over all of Philadelphia."

He paused to look out over the crowd. Their eyes were wide open with expressions of hunger. "I told y'all that it was a matter of time. I told y'all that we would be The New Untouchables. I told y'all that we gon' have it all." He raised his right fist in the air and raised his tone. *"It's Fifth Street time!"*

"Yeah," they hollered in response. Shit is going to get real hectic, Tyrone thought. The crowd held their guns and bottles of liquor in the air. Some were smoking weed and held up joints. They all started chanting, "Fifth Street, Fifth Street/ We can't be beat/ Fifth Street, Fifth Street/ We can't be beat/ Fifth Street, Fifth Street/ We can't be beat . . .." Tyrone felt that it was time for him to dip. The chaos was making him nervous.

Quadir started waved his hands in the air to calm the crowd down. "I want y'all to know that we are The New

Untouchables." They crowd nodded their heads, sipped their drinks and mentally counted the money that they were soon expecting to make. Quadir always provided them with plenty to drink and to get high with. They didn't know that he would let them make just enough money to keep them dependent on him. "We are going to be collecting money from everybody in the city. If they pimping, we get paid. If they selling heroin, we get paid. If they selling cocaine, we get paid. If they extortin', we get paid. If they running a gambling spot, *we get what?*"

"We get paid!" Tyrone was just about to get in his hoopty when he heard the crowd yelling. Quadir was about to become too powerful for his own good. He knew that it was time for him to go for self. All of what he just saw meant that when Quadir took over, there was going to be major chaos. Tyrone didn't want any part of that.

"The Feds told you that I'm the number two man in The Untouchables. They also told you that I was indicted. They also told you that there is a $500,000 reward on my head. It has been five days. They haven't come to get me."

When they would come had been on Fifth Street's collective mind and a constant issue of concern. Quadir had refused to go into hiding. For a few days he had stood outside of the projects, letting himself be seen.

"Let me tell you why they haven't come up in here. *They fear Fifth Street!* All of Philadelphia *fears Fifth Street!*"

Some of them started making noise. Others were so drunk from that statement that they could only nod their heads. They had never thought they had so much power. Quadir knew exactly what to do to make them feel good. He wanted to make them feel like they were invincible.

"I know that Fifth Street has mad love for Quadir. They know Fifth Street has mad love for Quadir. Philadelphia knows Fifth Street has mad love for Quadir. That's why Quadir isn't scared of the Feds." Quadir laughed a little as he said this last sentence.

He wanted to let the people know that he had faith that they would protect him, no matter what and that he would provide them with all the things they wanted to get from the streets. He was their leader and he had them hypnotized.

"Yeah," they started hollering before chanting some more. "Fifth Street, Fifth Street/ We can't be beat/ Fifth Street, Fifth Street/ We can't be beat . . .." For about three minutes they hollered and made noise. Quadir just watched and grinned. There were only a few more moves for him to make to execute his plan. Once he went into hiding and let it be known, he just had to get rid of Alvin and fake his death. From there he could rule the city without ever being seen. For years, he taught and instilled loyalty into his clique. They were ready and didn't mind worshiping him.

Quadir didn't mind waiting for the crowd to calm down. It was their time. He figured Tyrone was somewhere about to put another needle in his arm. Soon Quadir would send his people after him. Maybe the sooner he killed Tyrone, the better. When the crowd stopped making noise, Quadir sold them more dreams.

"There isn't a man in this room that isn't going to be a millionaire. That's how much respect Fifth Street has in the streets. There isn't going to be a damn thing that y'all can't buy. Ain't nobody in the city going to testify against Fifth Street. Just like for decades, nobody would testify against The Untouchables. *We're The New Untouchables!*"

"Yeah," somebody yelled, "The New Untouchables!"

"The Untouchables have fallen apart because of that bitch Stacy. The bitch got weak and she was only locked up for a week. Jimmy put his life on the line for her and ended up dead." He pointed to a sheet that covered some washing machines. An assistant lifted the sheet to reveal Jimmy's dead body. "He got killed for a bitch that wouldn't even give him any pussy."

The crowd was stunned. It didn't take long for them to figure out that Quadir had killed Jimmy because he had taken Stacy's side. If he would kill an Untouchable, then he would certainly kill one of them. Fear had them not knowing how to react.

"He didn't have to die. He placed a no-good bitch before his clique. No bitches will be allowed in this clique. Not Fifth Street." Many of the men in those projects were admirers of Stacy because of her reputation and her rap single, "I'm Bangin' 'Em." Some of them wanted to fuck her. Some had even more respect for her after they found out she was a member of The Untouchables.

Quadir continued. "This is the only mistake The Untouchables ever made. It's the same mistake that Sampson made, the same mistake Solomon made—fucking with the wrong bitch." These were the same stories he had been planting in their heads for years. By their reactions, he could see that they felt what he was saying, though they weren't excited. He'd purposely hit them with Stacy and Jimmy to make a low point for his speech, and to instill fear in their hearts. He also wanted them to think that they were with the baddest clique in the land and smart for being down.

"The Untouchables didn't have any problems before that bitch got locked up." It was the second to last phase of his speech. It was time to rally them back up. "Until that bitch got locked up, nobody knew the identities of The Untouchables."

A yellow cab had stopped in front of the Fifth Street Projects. There were two occupants in the back. They had gotten dressed in the cab in heavy black leather outfits and were covered from head to toe.

In the basement the only thing that could be heard was Quadir. "There are only four Untouchables left. Two are still real and true to the game. One is a rat, and one is harboring a rat. We are The New Untouchables and things are going to be different. None of us are going to get weak for a bitch. Bitches are going to be ruled and told what to do."

Two more cabs pulled up. One was green and the other was purple. All of the occupants had on the same attire and were communicating with their own scrambled cell phone network.

The members from the yellow cab got out first. From under their leather jackets they pulled out their Uzis and placed them behind their backs. With weapons out and bulletproof helmets on their heads, they approached the first building. The other members from the other cabs weren't far behind.

"Fifth Street, Fifth Street/ We can't be beat/ Fifth Street, Fifth Street/ We can't be beat!" Quadir had made them see the light. They were ready to go out and kill Stacy and Alvin. Quadir's plan was to flush Stacy and Alvin out by blowing up everything that belonged to them. The first stop was going to be Stacy's drug spot on 10th Street. In less than an hour, Quadir planned to have his peeps rob the place, kill everyone inside and burn it down.

Just outside the building there were two cats on guard duty. They noticed the cats with the leather outfits. They didn't feel threatened, but they were not going to let them walk around the projects unchecked. "Yo, weirdo, stop. This is the Fifth Street Projects. You and your friends need to get the fuck out of here."

They just kept walking.

"One more step and I'm going to fill y'all up with holes," the guard hollered as he pointed his nine millimeter pointed at them. His partner had his gun pointed also. "Fuck it then." He pulled the trigger.

Boom! Boom! Boom! The fire from the nines lit up the night. It was a regular thing in the Fifth Street Projects, so people didn't look out of their windows immediately.

When the bullets hit them, the duo stopped walking for a few seconds. The bullets fell to the ground with slight clinks.

"Holy shit! Did you see that? I know I shot the tall one. I don't miss when I haven't been drinking," the first soldier said to the other.

"Shoot at their heads," the other guard said.

When the bullets bounced off the see-through part of the helmets, the guards got scared. They hadn't been trained for what to do in such a situation. Before they knew it their legs had been shot up from an Uzi. They hadn't heard a sound.

"Tell us where Quadir is at before we kill you." One of the leather-clad people held the guard by the throat and pointing the Uzi at his nuts. The guard wanted to play tough. "OK tough guy." A shot went off.

"Oh, shit! That was my nuts," the guard hollered out. "Don't kill me. He's downstairs having a meeting." The guard figured he could save his life and send the assassin to his death.

The first assassin said, "Kill this no good piece of shit." The second pulled out a knife and cut the first guard's throat, then the other's. Two more cabs pulled up just as they had gathered at the entrance. Stacy was in the last cab.

"Yes, we are going to finish off Stacy and Alvin. Then Philadelphia belongs to who?"

"Belongs to Fifth Street."

"Belongs to who?"

"Belongs to Fifth Street!"

Stacy was on the steps with the eight trained assassins. "Let's do this," she said through her helmet. "When the doors are kicked in, we walk in as planned and keep firing. Just don't shoot Quadir. He's mine." They all nodded.

Quadir wanted to hear the chant one more time before he sent them on their missions. In the morning he planned to wake up to the news of his work. "Let me know who the fuck we are one more time."

"Fifth Street, Fifth Street/ We can't be beat/ Fifth Street, Fifth Street/ We can't be—"

All eyes turned to the doors as they burst open. The guards that were standing in front of the doors got hit with bullets first. The rat-tat-tat, rat-tat-tat, rat-tat-tat of machine gun fire and cats hollering, were the only sounds. Blood was everywhere before many could realize what was happening. The assassins recognized Quadir on the milk crates and were careful not to shoot him. They took the perimeter as they all rushed into the room. Some of Fifth Street were far enough from the action to pull their weapons. They had no choice but to shoot back or get up under a dead body. The gunfire went on for about ten minutes. The assassins had orders to leave no one standing except Quadir. He didn't move an inch. He wasn't the kind of cat to get scared. His arrogance wouldn't have let him reveal his fear, anyway. He recognized the shortest figure as Stacy.

Once the Fifth Street members were either laid out or had stopped firing their weapons, Stacy ordered her peeps to cease fire. She looked over the bodies to see if any one of them might be able to grab a weapon. Many of them were screaming from the pain of multiple shots to the body and head.

"So you had to go and kill Jimmy along with kidnapping my son and mother," Stacy said to Quadir as she removed her helmet. She wanted him to know that it was she.

"You are a rat and you got what you deserved." Those were just words. He didn't care if he wasn't making any sense.

"Please don't say that I'm a rat again."

"You's a rat and you know it. We didn't get indicted until you got arrested." A few seconds later he yelled, "Oh shit," and grabbed his right knee.

"I'm going to shoot you in the balls the next time. I think that your ass is the rat. You the one that want to be in Alvin's spot badder than anything in life. I really think that you the rat."

Quadir's pride kept him from making any more noise because of his knee. "OK, let's get the discovery from the federal prosecutors and find out who is the rat."

"Never that. I'm not going to let you live. This isn't about you being a rat. It's about you kidnapping my son."

Quadir chose to say nothing.

"Good night. I'll be out of the country and your greedy ass is going to be dead. Don't worry, I'm going to get Tyrone before I leave town."

"I knew I should have stopped Alvin from letting you in The Untouchables. You done messed up The Untouchables."

"No, *you* messed up The Untouchables when you fucked with my baby. Now shut the fuck up and take this!" Stacy pulled the trigger and aimed up and down his body. When the partial clip ran out, she pulled out another one and finished riddling his body with bullets. When she was done, Quadir had no less than one hundred fifty bullets in his body. His face was unrecognizable. "I mI'm bangin' 'em," she yelled before she left.

<u>Chapter Twelve</u>

Thursday, August 31
It was one o'clock in the morning when Spanks made it to the Fifth Street Projects, two hours after the crime.

"What the fuck happened here?" Spanks asked Matthews. Matthews had walked up to him a few seconds after he got out the car.

"Well. It's simple and sophisticated." Matthews was extremely happy to see the anguish on Spanks' face. His intention was to drag the ordeal out as long as he could. "Somebody or some people killed most of the Fifth Street Projects' thugs. There are about one hundred dead bodies in the basement." He purposely held back information.

"Are you fucking trying to be funny with me? *Tell* me about Quadir and Jimmy!" If there hadn't been any involvement with The Untouchables, Spanks wouldn't have been out there in the middle of the night.

"They haven't finished pulling bodies out of there." Matthews knew the answer. He was glad to see Spanks' plan blow up in his face. Spanks had his men and the National Guard ready to go in at six o'clock in the morning. Matthews was one of the first ones on the scene. The first thing he did was look for Quadir and other members of The Untouchables amongst the bodies.

"Are you telling me that you are the Special Agent in- Charge and you don't know what is going on?" Spanks counted the body bags that the rescue team and fire fighters were bringing out, back-to-back. It seemed like all the people from the projects were in the yard. Mothers wanted to see if their sons had been killed.

"There was a big shoot-out in the basement laundry room."

"A shoot-out in a basement? A shoot-out between whom?" It wasn't making sense to Spanks. "Nobody has shoot-outs in basements."

"Yeah, some people in black came through and shot up all of the Fifth Street Gang." Matthews loved that he could tell this incredible story that wasn't going to harm him. He was still glad that this took place because of work that he had put in.

"You aren't going to tell me that none of those people in black didn't get shot-up or killed." Spanks' expression clearly stated that he didn't want to catch Matthews in a lie.

Matthews wanted to laugh. Spanks' plans had been totally fucked up. "Well, we haven't found anybody in large black outfits that were killed or wounded. The witnesses say they had on helmets." Might as well add that to the fire. Matthews wondered what Spanks was going to do.

"I want to see what it looks like down there." They started walking. "There is only one man in this town that is sophisticated enough to pull off a massacre like this, and massacre is what it is. I have never seen so many body bags at one time." He didn't give a damn about the dead bodies. He cared about how embarrassing this was going to be to his reputation: as a federal agent he didn't want it known that he couldn't arrest a suspect that was right under his nose.

"Whoever did this, sir, made sure that there would be no survivors or witnesses."

Spanks' look told Matthews to save it. They kept walking toward the building.

Matthews really didn't care. He was enjoying every bit of this mess. This is what you get for taking over my case. He knew that the people in Washington and the higher-ups in Philadelphia were going to be mad at Spanks.

Spanks thought to himself that he should have pushed the operation up by one day. No matter, there would have been major risk. His only consolation was that he wasn't as embarrassed with the present situation as he would have been if he had gone in and didn't deliver Quadir. If Quadir was dead—then he could just go to plan B without hesitation.

"Damn this place looks like a hell hole," Spanks exclaimed as he walked through the laundry room door. Bloody and battered bodies were scattered all over the room and over a thousand gun shells adorned the floor. The smell of fresh blood still lingered in the air, causing Spanks to feel a little sick. "I've never seen so many gun shells in my life." Gazing at the faces of the lifeless bodies Spanks saw that most of them were kids and teenagers. "Look at this shit! There are kids everywhere! What is that body doing over there on the washing machines?" The paramedics and firemen had only taken out about fifty bodies and hadn't crossed the room.

"I'm not sure. I didn't go over there. I didn't want to mess up the crime scene." Which was a straight lie.

Spanks walked around the perimeter of the room. "There's too much of a crime scene to mess up." He would have walked straight across the room, but he didn't want to take a chance of falling down in the middle of a bunch of dead bodies. "This is exactly who I thought it would be. Jimmy." He was trying to make himself sound like a genius.

Matthews knew this. "I wonder how he ended up under that sheet?" Might as well have some more fun.

"What the fuck does it matter?" Spanks retorted as he turned around. "I bet that's Quadir there. He was standing on those milk crates and holding a meeting. I recognize the military jacket and kufi. I bet he has on a bulletproof vest. I've been watching him for years. He loves to hide behind young kids. What a waste of intelligence."

"Sounds like you are on point." Matthews' tone was slightly sarcastic with a bit of jest.

Spanks wasn't paying any attention. "Damn, two Untouchables were murdered in the same building. The news is going to love this." He walked back toward the door on the same path. "What doesn't make sense to me is why Tyrone isn't here."

"I guess you have a point there." It was nice to see Spanks perplexed again. Matthews tried to think of a way of getting his case back, or at least getting credit for breaking The Untouchables.

"This has got to be the work of Alvin and Stacy. They must have felt that Quadir was a rat and/or Stacy wanted revenge for the kidnapping."

It was time to be the devil's advocate. "That had to be one hell of a chance to take, especially since she has her son and mother back. Anybody could have seen her and wanted the reward. Everybody in Philadelphia knows what she looks like. They all know Alvin, also."

"Shit, I heard about people killing other people right in front of police officers because of their kids. A mother's love can be one hell of a thing." Spanks knew that he was on a roll. He could see the prosecutor using the massacre at the federal trial. It would make great evidence. There had to be a way to tie the murder to Alvin and Stacy.

"I don't know. Stacy couldn't have done this by herself. Alvin surely didn't: he's in a wheelchair. This could be someone that we don't know about." Matthews wanted to put some doubt in Spanks' mind. His gut told him that Stacy had something to do with it. It was the kind of move The Untouchables were known to make: in and out, without a trace. They had started walking back upstairs.

"If they didn't do it, then they might as well have done it. We just have to catch Alvin, Stacy and Tyrone. It's over for The Untouchables."

That wasn't what Matthews wanted to hear. "So what is our next move?" He wanted Spanks to think that he was with him. There was no doubt in Matthews' mind that Alvin was going to make it out of the country, if he hadn't already left yet. They exited the building.

"I'm getting ready to show you how the Feds get down when we really want to get our man." They were almost to Spanks' car. Spanks had a big smile on his face.

"Oh yeah," Matthew commented with a fake smile on his face. Matthews thought that Spanks had to be acting cocky because of the pressure that was about to come down. He couldn't believe there was a good reason for Spanks to have found some energy from somewhere and really felt as good as he sounded.

"By the morning, Stacy's mother is going to be arrested for money laundering." Spanks opened his car door and got in.

Matthews wanted to laugh, but decided to hold it in. He knew there was no evidence against Stacy's mother. "How are we supposed to do that?"

Spanks cranked up his engine. "Get ready to go out to the mansion at six o'clock, like in a few hours. I'll have a search warrant and arrest warrant on your desk in two hours." Spanks was just waiting for Matthews to say that he understood what to do before he put his car in drive.

Matthews wanted to say that six o'clock was in a few hours. "Are you sure about this?"

"You damn right I'm sure. Oh, yeah: her father gets out of prison on Monday. Serve him also. We have evidence on him. *Just handle it.*" The window went up and the car was in motion.

Chapter Thirteen

The only thing that would have made Alvin happier was also having Tyrone murdered. This meant that there would be no more loose ends. He also wanted Tyrone done because he felt that Tyrone had something to do with Jimmy's murder. Instead of letting his lust for revenge dictate, Alvin felt it was best to leave the country as planned.

For almost thirty years straight Alvin made sure he watched, or at least listened to, the morning news that came on at six o'clock. This morning was going to be really special. Last night's work had to be the first thing on the news. It would be like the last episode in his criminal career. It made him feel good that he would be going down in history as Mr. Untouchable. For decades, no one could say for sure that he was Mr. Untouchable, though his power was felt, feared and and respected. He had lived out the vision that he had in his mind.

Alvin coughed a bit when the cigar smoke hit his lungs. The coughing was bothering him less and less. A big sip of Hennessy made him feel like there was nothing wrong. Alvin smoked hard and drank hard when he wanted to think hard. In ten minutes the news would be on.

In less than six hours he planned to be on a private plane headed for Cuba. From there, he and his crew would make their way to Malaysia by plane, train or whatever transportation that seemed the safest. The last thing that Alvin wanted to do was have a child before he died. It was the only thing that had eluded him. He felt that a son would make his life complete, something that he could leave on this earth. That would be his first mission when he got to Malaysia. His desire to have a son was that more intense since he had learned of Jimmy's murder. He had treated Jimmy just like he was his son. In five more minutes the news would be on.

The second thing Alvin wanted to do was write a book about how he had made himself Untouchable. There was no doubt in his mind that many publishers would be interested. There was no need to let someone else try to write his story. He wanted the public to know all the details from the source. Most of all, Alvin wanted to see Stacy get out of the game without having to look back. He didn't want her to be on the run for the rest of her life. It wouldn't be good for her, her son and mother. Plus she wouldn't be able to use her lyrical talents the way she was supposed to. Which one he wanted to do the most, though, he couldn't figure out. Thirty seconds before the news came on.

Alvin thought how nice it would be to have Stacy sitting beside him. If she hadn't done so much last night, he would have woken her up. Watching the news again at nine o'clock with her would be cool. He poured himself a drink and took a big sip to put him in the mood for the show. The cameraman had just closed in on the reporter.

"We have a special live broadcast this morning. We now go directly to our correspondent. Mr. Sneed, how are you doing this morning?"

"I'm good, and we are bringing you the latest in the investigation of The Untouchables. Here with me now is Special Agent Mark Matthews of the Drug Enforcement Administration. Special Agent Matthews, would you please tell us what is happening here?"

Alvin noted that the scenery in the back looked familiar.

"Behind us is one of the mansions that belong to the leader of The Untouchables, Alvin Jones. As you can see, my men are taking out all the furniture, sculptures and all the other valuables." Matthews was dressed in a brand new suit and tie. This situation made him feel like he was in charge of the case again.

Alvin laughed. His lawyer had already hipped him to putting his properties and businesses in the names of corporations formed in places that used secrecy laws. He knew there was no way they could trace the mansion back to him or any illegal activity. His lawyers would take care of it. A Jewish law firm had been hired to handle it.

"So you say that this beautiful mansion belongs to Alvin Jones, the leader of The Untouchables?"

"Yes, it does," Matthews responded proudly. "And it's about to belong to the federal government."

"Aren't Mr. Jones and a few others under indictment? Don't they also have outstanding warrants and rewards for their arrest?" There was nothing like good questions to put the police on the spot in front of the public, especially a federal law enforcement official.

Alvin murmured, "You can just forget about me. And forget about finding me, Mr. Matthews. I'm about to be gon' till November."

Matthews was still smiling. "He and his whole gang are in hiding. We are looking to get them any day. In the meantime, as we seize this mansion, we are going to arrest a member of The Untouchables." Alvin leaned closer. He was expecting to hear something about them busting Tyrone's door down. "Mrs. Kellis Dee is being arrested today on charges of money laundering. My men will be bringing her out in a minute."

"Ain't that a bitch! They're arresting Stacy's mother," Alvin said out loud. Alvin wanted to get Stacy so that she could see it. He figured that by the time he did that, the program would be off. Time to think is also what he needed and wanted. The sight of them bringing Mrs. Dee out of his mansion made him chew on his cigar and grind his back teeth. Whenever something happened because of The Untouchables, it offended Alvin, especially on the day that he was planning to leave the country. There was no way that he was going to let Matthews beat him like this.

"Damn," Stacy hollered when she saw her mother, in handcuffs, being escorted by DEA agents. "What the fuck are they arresting my mother for? She ain't a member of shit and she ain't done shit. You should have gotten me up earlier, Alvin."

Alvin was just as pissed off as she was. Instead of talking, he just sipped on his drink and tried to find an idea to solve all the problems that were coming down.

"Them motherfuckers took your house, and arrested my mother for money laundering." Stacy looked back at Alvin to see what he had to say. "I bet my child is at Social Services.

"Be cool, Stacy. We are going to figure this out, just like we've been making moves for the past five years."

"We ain't leaving the country," Stacy stood and paced about the room, "not without my mother and son. Plus, my dad is getting out on Monday." She didn't want to push Alvin by asking him if he was with her. She wanted him to say it but Alvin just sat there like he wasn't listening. "Damn, Alvin! Say something!"

"I told you to be cool. Didn't you burn up enough energy last night?"

Alvin would say something like that at a time like this. "I can't believe that them bastards have my mother! At least, they are going to have to give her bail." They couldn't pull the same trick on her mother that they had pulled on her. This thought made Stacy feel that the situation could be easily resolved and they could all skip the country as planned. "I just have to find my son and have Jesse pick him up. Jesse can just say that he's the father." Jesse and Devon hadn't met each other yet. "Alvin, please say something." Stacy knelt in front of him.

Alvin didn't want to say a thing. If it had been anyone else, he would have kept his mouth shut. "I'm going to have to leave to make a few calls." No one was allowed to make phone calls on cell phones from the hideout. "I'm sure she'll be able to make bail. In case they don't give her a bail, I'm going to have a Plan B." Alvin took a sip of his drink because he felt a cough coming on.

Stacy stood, turned around and and smiled. She didn't want Alvin to see her expression. She felt good just from hearing that he was planning on handling the situation. "What do you mean, if she doesn't get a bail? What are we going to do then?" Her mother and son were on the line. She wanted to know what Alvin had on his mind.

It was nice to hear Stacy change her tone and demeanor. "I can't tell you just yet. I'm going to have to work out the details this evening." Evening meant that it wouldn't be dark for at least an hour.

"Since when have you started keeping secrets from me? At least in this situation, I want to be ready to do what we got to do. Plus, I need to put Jesse to the test. So tell me, Alvin." As of yet, Stacy hadn't seen Alvin fail. It wasn't a matter of faith; it was a matter of curiosity and sensitive emotions.

"Baby girl, you are just like my daughter. It's a must that I do right by you." He quickly placed his fist in front of his mouth to catch his cough. His whole body leaned as he coughed hard, three times. Stacy ran behind him and rubbed his back. She wanted to tell him to go see a doctor, but there was no need to say something that was practically impossible. "I feel that I got to do right by you. You and Jimmy have been the best bulls that I had in the streets."

"What the fuck are you talking about? I don't like the way that you are talking."

"I'm just trying to tell you how much I love you, Stacy. I should have made you my lady when I had the chance, before

Jesse came in the picture. It's always been business before pleasure for me." The look on Alvin face was one of sincerity and relief.

"Why are you getting like this on me?" Stacy had thought the same things; back in the day Alvin had paid her good money to spend the weekends with him. He had also had her to do a lot of errands for which he paid her well. "This ain't the time, Alvin. It ain't like you are getting ready to die or something."

Alvin really wanted to tell Stacy that he was in love with her. Her gangster attitude had kept him intrigued since he had decided to give her a small piece of work. She turned out to be that ambitious, focused, determined and disciplined female that he had been looking for all his life. "Baby, I just needed to make a small confession. It wasn't an Usher confession."

"Well, I love you, too." Stacy laughed. She had always told Alvin that she had love for him. For him to say what he was saying now was making her wonder what he was going to say next. "So, all this love means that you can tell me about Plan B."

"Nah, I can't tell you that, just yet. I can tell you that it has something to do with the promise that you made." He wanted to have her fully prepared to do what he wanted her to do. He could tell her at least this much.

"OK, maybe I can make you tell me something by telling you something." Giving wasn't her style, at all.

Alvin laughed before he took another pull of his cigar. He knew there was nothing Stacy could say that would make him change his mind. They just stared at each other, with smirks on their faces. "Go on try, little girl," he challenged as he laughed.

Stacy considered changing her mind. There was the possibility that this wasn't the right time. "Nah, I ain't gon' tell you."

"So, the little girl has ran out of heart." It was a good time to tease her like he had always done. Alvin laughed hard, thinking that this might be that time that she didn't step up to the batter's box.

"So, you call yourself challenging me?" Stacy's tone was gritty even was she smirked.

Alvin sipped on his drink so that he could think of something to push her buttons. "Well, you call it what you like. I didn't change my mind about sayin' something. You did. I got you." There was no doubt this would get to her.

"Nah, I ain't going for that. You tell me the plan and what I promised to do. Then, I'll tell you what's on my mind." Stacy felt like she had some leverage on him.

"No, I ain't going for that. You're game is good; I'm just too good of a player to go for it. Think of something else." Alvin turned his chair around and headed toward the kitchen.

What do you do Stacy? Fuck it; might as well go for it. "Devon is *your son!*"

Alvin stopped just as he was about to downstroke his wheels. It was a comment that he couldn't ignore. Plus, it wasn't like Stacy to lie. Slowly, he turned around. "I know you don't want to know that bad?"

"I'm telling you the truth." Her arms were now crossed. For years she wanted to tell him, but she kept putting it off because of the risk of having to tell him how it happened.

"Curiosity has really got the best of you. I can't blame you, because I've always told you what you wanted to know if you were involved. This time I can't do that, yet." Alvin would dismiss the fact that she had played with his feelings, for he had never told her how he felt about having a son. He started wheeling his chair back around.

"I might as well tell you now. You need to know this." Stacy was putting things off to make sure that she maintained his attention. Alvin turned to look at her. His expression said that he was about to get pissed off. "I'm going to tell you some really gully shit." She bit her lips.

"This had better be good, Stacy." Alvin faced her.

"I put holes in some of the condoms we used." She paused to let this sink in. "Before you say anything, I switched condoms when you weren't looking. I didn't mean no harm. I have his DNA test at home." Stacy hoped that Alvin wouldn't yell at her for very long.

He turned his wheelchair and left—no words or looking back.

Stacy had to lay down and collect her thoughts. She had said what she had said to make sure that he felt the same way about her son and mother as she did. There was no way she was going to let the Feds put her mother in jail. It might have been the best time or the worst time to tell Alvin that he was Devon's father. Alvin's talk about leaving the country and retiring as soon as possible was getting to her. She didn't want him to rectify the situation from a distance. Moves had to be made immediately. Making Alvin love Devon more than he already did was a way to make sure that he stayed the course. Maybe he wouldn't be mad that long. Having to wait eleven hours before leaving the spot was also bothering her. There was no room for mistakes.

"So why did you do it," Alvin asked as he rolled up quietly.

Stacy was caught off guard. She was practically in a daze. "I didn't want you to bail out and leave me here to handle the situation by myself. I need you, Alvin."

"I didn't mean that! Why did you trick me?"

"Oh, that." Explaining herself was the biggest factor that kept Stacy quiet about the situation. That act of gulliness could spoil her entire reputation and street credibility, after it had taken her so long to gain respect. There was just too much at risk. "I needed you to take care of me. I needed you to stop me from sinking." It had all worked out, just not as planned; Alvin was the one that helped her get rich. It was just like he was taking care of his son.

"I'm going to forgive you. Make sure you get with Jalissa tonight and get your mother a bond. I'll see some people to put Plan B in effect. Also, I'll find where your son is at, in case Jalissa doesn't know." There was plenty of reason for him to be mad. Being tricked was something that he didn't take lightly. He understood because Stacy was on dope at the time. All that she had done was more than enough to make up for the situation. Plus, now, he had a son.

"OK." A smile came across her face, making her dimples show. When Alvin rolled away, she looked up and sent a silent "thank you" to God with her hands and lips. "I love you, Alvin."

"I love you too, Stacy."

Chapter Fourteen

"You can make this really easy on yourself, Mrs. Dee." Spanks could barely sleep the night before. Closing in on The Untouchables had him extremely excited. "We really don't want to do this to you. It's Alvin that we want." He also wanted to say Stacy, but it was too early to go there yet.

"I ain't done nothin' and I don't know nothin'." Mrs. Dee was a tough old lady. Life in South Philly and dealing with her husband, who couldn't stay out of trouble, had made her tough.

Old lady or no old lady, Spanks wasn't going to be nice. "I know that you are a grandmother and you don't want to go to jail." Matthews stood in the back of the room and thought that the old lady wasn't going to budge because of intimidation. "I don't have a problem putting you in jail and making sure you rot there until you die."

Mrs. Dee was in her mid-fifties and in decent health. With her figure long gone and her husband doing time, her life was centered around her grandchild and helping Stacy handle her businesses. Her husband had told her how nasty the cops could be when they interrogated a person.

"You can sit there like you are innocent, if you like. There is only one person that's going to be able to help you and that's you. Stacy is on the run or in hiding. Your husband is going to get arrested when he walks out the door of the state penitentiary."

Mrs. Dee thought that this man couldn't be serious about putting her in jail. Because she still had on her street clothes, she felt there was a chance they would just let her go if she didn't act scared. Being quiet was her way of concealing her fear. Never had she been through anything with the police, or had she thought she would ever get arrested.

"The last thing you want to be is quiet." Spanks had propped his feet up on the desk. With a smirk on his face, he looked Mrs. Dee straight in the eye and plopped a package of papers on his desk. "There's enough evidence here to get you an easy ten years in prison."

Mrs. Dee wanted to say something but using different words to say that she didn't do anything would have made her feel silly. Pride kept her from taking that risk, though curiosity made her want to ask. Her faith in Stacy made it easy for her to hold steadfast.

Matthews knew that he would come up with a better approach to the situation.

"Fuck this bitch! She wants her old ass to go to jail." Spanks stomped out the room and slammed the door.

Mrs. Dee jumped a little when the door slammed. Then she relaxed in her chair, thinking that she was alone. She wondered where they could be keeping her grandson. She disliked that Devon had seen her in handcuffs. To make matters worse, there was nothing she could do about it except tell him to stop crying. Making bail is what she hoped for if they decided to give her some bogus charges.

A minute had been long enough to let her relax. Time to move in. Matthews pulled a chair up next to her and sat down. "You can relax, Mrs. Dee. Don't let that mean guy scare you."

"I'm not scared." Her instincts to hide her fear made her speak before she realized it. This officer was the first one to act friendly toward her since she had been arrested. It was a nice thing.

Matthews smiled a little bit harder. "I know that you aren't scared. You really shouldn't be here." He had been taught to make it sound like he was on the suspect's side. Psychology was half the game.

"So what are they trying to charge me with?"

With a sympathetic voice, Matthews eased it on her. "Well, it's one of our simpler charges. It's called money laundering." Matthews gave her this information to make her ask more questions and continue to talk.

"What is money . . . laundering?" She said it slow to make sure she was saying it right.

"Well, it's one of those charges they use when there is nothing else that they can use."

"Does that mean that I'm going to be all right?" Mrs. Dee hoped to hear him say something comforting.

This was going exactly where Matthews wanted it . "Well, it means that you may have to do a maximum of twenty years."

Mrs. Dee wanted to believe the twenty-year figure instead of the ten-year figure, though it was way more time, because she didn't dislike Matthews like she disliked Spanks. Still she remained silent. There was nothing she could think to say without showing a sign of weakness.

Matthews could see the softening in her eyes. "All you have to do is tell us all that you know about Alvin and The Untouchables." He wouldn't allude to her saying anything about her daughter until it was the last thing he could say, or until she acted really weak.

The last thing Mrs. Dee was going to do was give them information. She hated rats more than her husband. "I don't know a thing." This statement slipped out because she felt offended.

"We know about all the money you deposited in Stacy's businesses. It's a crime." He tried his best preacher impersonation.

"Handling money isn't a crime. That was my daughter's money that I put into those businesses." Mrs. Dee didn't know that she had just pleaded guilty to some of the elements of money laundering.

Maybe we should have gone after the mother first. "Money laundering is as simple as putting illegally gained money in a bank." Matthews pushed her to act more defensively. He knew that the more she said, the worse it would be for her.

"You can't be serious! My daughter didn't earn all of her money illegally." Mrs. Dee didn't know what the law was and thought she was saying the right thing.

"I ain't through with this old bitch yet," Spanks yelled as he entered the room. "She doesn't know that she's fucking with the DEA and the federal government. We lock up old people too."

The tone of his voice made Mrs. Dee jump. It reminded her of her husband yelling at her. She couldn't relax. The thought of going to jail because of just spending money had her thrown off.

"In the last two years, you deposited over a million dollars into several businesses that we know belong to Stacy. You, and only you, will be doing twenty years. This is the evidence." His right hand caressed the package on the table.

Mrs. Dee was stunned and confused.

Another special agent knocked on the door before entering. "Her lawyer is here and wants to see her."

"Fuck it," Spanks responded. "We read her her rights before we told her about the time and crime of money laundering." Though they hadn't read her her rights, they would testify that they had, if necessary. Part of the game: their word against hers.

* * * *

Saturday September. 2
It took a day for Jalissa and Stacy to finally be able to talk on the phone. Jalissa didn't want to chance that the Feds were watching her and getting caught with Stacy. Getting caught meeting with a fugitive would look bad for an officer of the court.

"Damn, girl, why you put me off for a whole day? Don't I pay my lawyer bills on time?" Stacy had to say something just to maintain respect.

"You know how that go. A bitch be trippin' sometime." Jalissa played the conversation off so that the cab driver wouldn't be in her business. Placing the phone down, she told the cab driver to ride south on Broad Street. There were too many cops, of all kinds, within the city limits.

"So what's up with my son and mother?"

"He's fine; he will be coming home as soon as a parent picks him up." Jalissa had inquired about getting Devon herself. The supervisor of the group home had told her that there would be a conflict of interest because of her client. Jalissa knew it was the work of the Feds.

"So that means I can just go get my son?" Stacy knew that it couldn't be that simple.

"Don't even think about it. Remember, stick to the script," Jalissa warned Stacy.

"You think that I'm that stupid!" These were just words. Since Jalissa had told her, by phone, where her son was, Stacy had been thinking about going up in there and getting him.

"I know you, girl. You ain't slick." The cab had just hit the highway. Jalissa removed her scarf from her head.

"OK. Maybe I was thinking about paying my son a small

131

visit. I miss him. I know he misses me. You think it'll be OK to call over there?"

"Nah. I wouldn't do it. Why take the chance?" Jalissa made sure she kept up with the latest technology used by law enforcement.

"So you telling me that I can't see my son . . . till I don't know when!!" Stacy knew she was dead wrong for raising her voice at Jalissa.

"Calm down and think about everything that has been going on." Jalissa wanted to tell her that they had better leave the country if they didn't want to get life sentences. She would say it when the opportunity presented itself again.

"Tell me about my mother." The indictment really didn't matter at this point in the game. Stacy figured that with Quadir dead, there was no one to testify against The Untouchables. In her mind, the indictment would to be easy to handle.

"You know, the same ole bullshit. I got to get some money so I can go wash today. You know, when my mother was eighteen, she went to U.S.C from 1956 to 1957," Jalissa hinted, hoping that Stacy got it. She wanted Stacy to get familiar with the statutes. There was a chance that Stacy might go on the Internet and look them up. Stacy got the hints and became furious all over again.

"That's some bullshit. My mother hasn't committed a crime. You'll just beat that shit and she'll join me in Mexico." She rubbed her hands together like things were going to be easy.

"Not exactly." Stacy's expression changed. Jalissa broke eye contact and looked up and down the road. "Did I tell you that Neisha went to jail for putting stolen money in the bank?" Stacy's eyes were about to bulge out her head.

"You joking me." Stacy looked in the side view mirror to see if they were being followed.

"Yes, girl. They're planning on giving her ten years for Count One and a consecutive twenty years for Count Two." It was a relief to finally lay all the bad news on Stacy. Jalissa waited for Stacy to say something.

Stacy wasn't sure what to say. Ten, twenty, thirty years was a lot of time for her mother to do. She blamed herself because it was her money. "It's really that fucked up . . . they gon' do my momma dirty because they can't get to me."

"Yeah, cops said that they will let her go if she tells them whose money it was." It was a hell of a thing to have to tell a friend. If Stacy asked for her advice, Jalissa wasn't prepared to answer.

"Damn, Jalissa! You don't think that you can beat the charges?" Turning herself in to set her mother free wasn't something she wouldn't do without hesitation. Devon would at least have one of them with him. Letting the Feds have their way is what she would do only after there were no more options.

"I can fight it, girl, but there's too much evidence for Count One. She deposited over a million dollars in several accounts." Jalissa wished she had known what was happening with Stacy's money a long time ago. She could have schooled them on what was and wasn't illegal.

"I don't understand. It's just money." This was how most responded when they heard about a money laundering charge, especially when they or a family member was hit with it.

"They knew that she didn't have legal access to that kind of money. Plus, she had those businesses in her and her momma's names. That was her first mistake. Neisha's Jewelry and Neisha's Boutique; I mean come on everybody in the city knows who Neisha is."

"So, if we didn't have those businesses in our names, we'd be OK?" Alvin had schooled her on corporations after she had opened them. She figured that since they were The Untouchables, that it would never be a problem.

"With her and her mother having no-show jobs and her having her name on the buildings, the Feds went snooping." Jalissa knew it would be hard to prove that all of the big deposits were for legal business. $100,000 here, $20,000 there and $15,000 somewhere else made for an erratic deposit pattern.

"So she's going to lose if she goes to trial?"

"More than likely. I might beat Count Two because they haven't tried to make the money look legitimate. So count on her doing ten years."

"My momma can't do ten years!! I don't want my momma even doing one year." Stacy now wished she had left the country, and not gone after Quadir. He could have waited for later.

Jalissa hated to tell her partner what she had to say and paranoid that the Feds would come out of nowhere at any minute. "Maybe I'll be able to get her a reasonable bond. They are going to institute administrative forfeiture proceedings on Monday and freeze all of her accounts."

"Damn, maybe you'll get her a bond." Stacy began to wonder if Jalissa was still on her side. She had nothing but bad news and definitely had been talking to the Feds, a lot.

"Them motherfuckers are pulling all the strings they can to get her or her and/or the nigga she was working with. Girl, if they catch her, she'll be getting multiple life sentences. Her mother can do eight-and-a-half years. *She can't do a life sentence.*" An answer had materialized from the question she thought would come. Rationally it was the best decision, with the least amount of damages.

There was no argument for eight-and-a-half versus life. Leaving her mother just wouldn't be right. She would have to talk to Alvin. The entire time she thought that she was protecting her mother. If she could only talk to her Mother for a few minutes. "Damn, girl. This shit is serious."

"I know. I'm doing the best that I can do. You should take that trip you were talking about though. *Everybody*, including your ole bird, will understand."

"It's easy for you to make a decision. Your peeps aren't on the line." Stacy's face had turned beet red.

"Get off this exit, cabbie. I got to go, Baby Girl. I'm tellin' you to leave. I'll get Neisha's mom a good plea."

"What about my son?"

"I'll make sure he goes on vacation as well." Jalissa had her hand on the door handle, waiting for Stacy's last response. "I'll see if I can get her mother a good bond. I just know they aren't going to play fair."

Stacy let out a breath and responded, "OK."

Jalissa shut the door and ran down the block. The paranoia was killing Stacy. She needed to see Jesse.

* * * *

Desperation was something that Stacy wasn't used to feeling. Being trapped on FDC's eighth floor was one thing; her son and mother—and possibly her father—being trapped there was another thing. The bad news Jalissa had just laid on her made her think differently about the game. Getting her mother prison time because she was just handling money was a thought that never occurred to Stacy. She wondered had Alvin thought about this.

Her loneliness made her go to Jesse's mother's house. Miss Jacobs was the last person she wanted to see. The look Jesse's mother gave her always made her feel like she was out of place. Still, she had to go over there.

"Jesse, just hold me," Stacy said as she ran into his arms. He had been wanting to see her. The late night calls hadn't been enough. Getting by the Feds wasn't worth the risk. "Damn, you feel good." They had been embracing for almost a minute.

"Where do they have your son at, boo? I'll go get him." Jesse figured this was the best thing that he could say. He had been wanting to meet Devon for the longest.

"I don't want you to do that." Stacy knew there was nothing that he could do. They moved toward the bed and sat down. It felt good to her to be where they had made love passionately on so many occasions, for hours on end.

"I've been thinking about it and thinking about it," Jesse said. "I'll just tell them that I'm his father. It isn't like I'll be lying. We are going to be married after this." The situation felt awkward to him. He had to take some kind of action to help his lady.

"There is only one thing I need you to do." She pushed back on the bed. "Are you comfortable?" She smiled when he said yes.

"This is all that I need you to do." She placed her head on his chest and wrapped her arms around his back. Jesse held her and waited for Stacy to make the next move.

As the Gangsta Bitch she chose to become, Stacy had always known that death and doing time could be consequences of the game. Giving her life for her son, mother, father, respect or organization was something she would do on instinct, no questions asked. Having her mother and father doing time for her registered the same emotions. It wasn't their fault that they had enjoyed her money. She blamed herself for not knowing any better and putting them at risk.

As of yet, Jesse couldn't be consulted because he hadn't proven himself. Would he be able to deal with having a wife doing time—really doing a life sentence? Stacy wasn't ready to hear the answers to the questions. She had to put more thought to it before she talked to Jesse about it. With her doing a life sentence or several life sentences, how long would it be before he found himself another lady to fulfill his physical needs? Would she be able to deal with the news and rumors that her husband, or her fiancé, was in the streets with another female?

Jesse would have to visit her in prison. He certainly wouldn't be a secret anymore.

Stacy was sure that Jesse would say anything at the moment just to please her. Though she was glad to have the ring on her finger, she felt that his timing hadn't been the best. Trying to keep her desires and emotions from making the situation any more difficult was getting harder and harder. Having a good relationship with a man, especially a marriage, was conflicting with her Gangsta Bitch duties. She knew that she wasn't supposed to fall in love with a man that couldn't deal with the prices of the game. There was no time to test Jesse. The Feds were taking control of her life by the day. There was hardly any room to think or to make a mistake.

There was no choice but for Stacy to prepare for the worst-case scenario. Alvin had taught her to make a decision and stick with it—"Confusion is the soul's greatest weakness," he always said. If necessary, she was going to turn herself in to the Feds to let her mother go. Her father also, if he was arrested, unless she could get them out on bail. It was the only thing she could come up with, for Alvin was powerless against the Feds. By the time she had to do what she had to do, Alvin would be out of the country and safe.

Stacy also decided that would be the last time for her to embrace Jesse. All emotional ties had to be broken. While he was asleep, she left in the middle of the night. She left the engagement ring taped to the mirror with a note so that he couldn't miss it. The note read: "I can't be a wife to you and do a life sentence. Life means life in the Feds."

Triple Crown Publications presents

<u>Chapter Fifteen</u>

Sunday, September 3

Alvin had been up all night waiting for Stacy to come in. He couldn't help but wonder if the Feds had picked her up. So far, no bad news had come across the radio. Usually, she was back by two-thirty a.m. It was almost five o'clock and the sun would be up soon. When she came through the door, he was relieved.

When their eyes met, Stacy knew there were going to be a lot of questions. "So you waited up for me, Alvin." It wasn't going to be easy to avoid a conversation with him. She could see that he was very concerned.

"I've got something to tell you. But first I want to know if you are OK." Her body language and the ring missing from her finger told him that things had to have been rough on her.

"I'm OK. Jalissa gave me some really bad news." She sat on the couch next to him and removed her jacket. Him waiting up and being concerned was making her feel better. It dawned on her that Alvin had always been there for her.

"So, are you going to tell me what she told you?" Alvin wasn't smoking or drinking. All of the thinking and planning had been done.

"Jalissa told me that it might be best for me to skip the country. There is no doubt in her mind that my mother is going to do time." She put her head to her knees. Her hands were used as pillows.

Alvin already knew this. He knew that it would really affect Stacy in a negative manner. "So, what are you planning to do? Do you want to tell me?"

Stacy lifted her head. "What's up, Alvin? You ain't acting like yourself. You ain't drinking or smoking. I know you got something on your mind."

"I do have something on my mind. It may not be as good as what you have on your mind, especially since you don't have on your ring." No matter what she said, he was going to make her take his plan and run with it.

"I don't want my mother or father to do time for me. They've supported me all my life. Plus, they haven't been together in nine years." She wondered if she and Jesse could have a relationship while she did time? Would he make it for at least nine years?

"You know the federal government is going to give you a life sentence, or maybe more than one." Alvin's attorney had fully briefed him on what could happen to Stacy if she was apprehended. All knew she would be made an example of, especially since she was part of The Untouchables.

"I thought about that tonight." Stacy wanted to tell Alvin to shut up. Things were already bad enough.

"Word is that they are going to try to give you and I the death penalty if either of us gets caught." Alvin knew from instinct and from knowing her, that Stacy wanted to turn herself in, in exchange for her mother and father's freedom. He just wanted her to say it.

"You always told me that death could be a price for being in the game. Ain't that right?" She had raised her voice a bit. She wanted Alvin to leave the subject and her alone.

"Where is your ring at, Stacy?" Alvin raised his voice also to let her know that he was still the leader.

Stacy stood and walked to the other side of the room. Why is Alvin doing this to me? There was silence for over a minute.

"Talk to me, Stacy. I know Jesse hasn't changed his mind."

She still wouldn't say a thing. There was another minute of silence. She just kept looking up at the ceiling.

"I can guess. You gave him back the ring because you plan to turn yourself in to get your mother out."

Slowly, Stacy turned around. "Why can't you leave it alone? You ain't happy that I'm not going out like a rat and not letting my mother and father do a bid for me." The look on her face begged Alvin to leave her alone.

It was time to take her to the next phase. "What makes you think they are going to arrest your father?"

"Jalissa told me."

"What makes you think they can't get a bail?"

"I don't know. I just went through the bail thing. The Feds want us too bad. You know this." Saying these things made Stacy feel worse. She wanted to sleep so she could put the situation out of her mind for a while. "Why are you asking me these things? I know there is nothing you can do if they don't get a—"

"I have a solution."

She put her hands on her hips. "What kind of solution do you have?"

"Sit down, girl, and let me talk to you. I can see that you are in your feelings and hurt."

Stacy was mad enough to slap him. She could see it

happening in her mind. Still she sat down. The look on her face let Alvin know that she thought he was wasting her time.

"Little girl, you are young, beautiful, talented and a hell of a woman." He wanted to make her feel good before he hit her with his idea. "I love you, girl, because I know you would never let anybody down. You have always done the right thing."

Alvin could see that the harsh emotions were leaving her face. He continued. "There is no way that I would let you fall by yourself. This is my organization."

Stacy wanted to say something but it was better to wait. Plus, the suspense was killing her. She again wondered why he wasn't smoking and drinking.

"I'm the one to take all the responsibility and to make all the decisions. We should have retired last year when we talked about it. I can't let you take a fall like that. You are just twenty-two." Alvin stopped talking and looked up at the ceiling.

Whatever Alvin had to say, had to be really serious. She had never seen him act like this. Stacy didn't know what to say or think. It was best to let him take his time.

"Stacy," Alvin continued with an innocent look on his face. "Stacy, I want you to testify against me."

Did he just say what I think he just said? There is no way that he asked Stacy to be a rat.

"There is only one way that I can set you free from this. I just need you to testify against me. I'm the one they really want."

Damn, that's what he really asked me to do! It was a shock. It was something that Stacy couldn't even force herself to think about. There was no way that she could hurt Alvin. She got up and walked across the room.

It wasn't a surprise to Alvin that she was shocked and surprised. "There's a reason for this that you also need to know. I'm about to die, Stacy."

As her heart skipped beats, Stacy turned around to see if Alvin was really serious. He was dead serious.

* * * *

Monday, September 24

"Good morning, Mr. Dee. My name is Special Agent Spanks." Calvin Dee leaned back in his chair and looked up at Spanks. He had been sitting in the tiny dark room for over an hour. It hadn't been a good month and he was already back in jail. "I'm the head of the DEA in Philadelphia." Spanks always brought suspects to his office to show off his power.

"Mr. Spanks, I just got out of the Pennsylvania penitentiary—meaning that I have nothing to do with drugs. Please tell me why I'm here." They had let him get all the way to Philadelphia before arresting him. They wanted him to get a little taste of freedom.

Spanks grinned. "I haven't exactly thought about charging you with a drug charge." He was lying. In a superseding indictment a few weeks later, Spanks planned to charge Calvin Dee in his daughter's drug conspiracy. A little heat at a time. For the moment, it was time to play small games.

"Well, you need to charge me with something if you don't want to be charged with false arrest." Calvin had spent many hours in the penitentiary's law library. By instinct, he was trying to use the law to his advantage.

"What you know about the law means nothing to me. We are the federal government. We make the rules and break the rules." This was both a challenge and a message.

There was a look of surprise on Calvin's face. Ordinarily, what he threatened with regard to the law had earned him a certain amount of respect. Dealing with the federal government was something that he hadn't calculated. "What do you mean by break the rules?" Before his bid, he would have tried to act like a tough guy.

"We have intentions of bringing The Untouchables down. We don't care what we have to do to do that. You are about to become a casualty of this war, unless you join my side." Spanks thought that he had sounded rather eloquent. He really just wanted information from Calvin and for Calvin to convince his daughter to be a rat. There were also thoughts of having Calvin tell lies in court on Alvin.

Calvin laughed. "There is nothing you can charge me with. I've been in prison for nine years. This must be a joke."

Matthews and Spanks just stared at him while he got his laugh on. Being in power was a beautiful thing. At times it amazed Spanks that so few criminals understood how the federal government operated until it was too late.

Calvin didn't like the way they were grinning. The looks on their faces told Calvin that they were dead serious.

Spanks tapped a pencil on his desk for effect. "You are about to do another nine years in prison." It was time to have some fun.

"For what!!?"

Spanks and Matthews laughed. Together they said, "money laundering." When it was time to work together, they put their differences aside.

"I haven't laundered any money."

"OK, you are kind of right," Matthews said with a grin on his face. "But you did make a bank transaction with drug money. That's right up there with money laundering."

Calvin laughed back at them. What Matthews had just said didn't make any sense to him. He was thinking about the lawsuit he could file for false arrest.

"Your daughter has sent you approximately $150,000 in the past three years." Matthews had been waiting to get this part in. "We know that you have over $120,000 in the bank. Most of it came from Stacy. We have all the records."

Calvin could accept what they just said. It was all true. Because of experience in reading law cases, he knew how extensive an investigation could be. As far as the charge, he wasn't ready to accept that.

"I have heard about what the Feds can do, but never have I heard anything like that. I'm not about to believe that this charge is a real crime until I see it in writing." *They really want my daughter.* He hoped that his request would get himself and his wife bail.

"Mr. Dee, we thought you would take such an attitude." Spanks slid him a manila folder.

Calvin took the folder and before he opened it, up he looked up at them to check their expressions. They were still dead serious. 18 U.S.C. 1957 said that a person that knowingly engages in a monetary transaction with criminally derived property of a value greater than $10,000 . . . is subject to up to ten years in prison.

"I haven't had any illegal money," Calvin said proudly. Saying that he hadn't deposited the money wasn't going to work. They had concrete evidence. Might as well see what is up with the rest of their case.

"Listen, Mr. Dee," Spanks said with a salesman's smile. "We have copies of many of the letters that you and your daughter wrote to each other. We also have tapes of your phone calls." A moment was needed to let this sink in.

My daughter must really be a member of The Untouchables. She could have told me something on a visit. She didn't even tell me that she was being protected by The Untouchables. What the fuck are they going to ask or tell me next? Testifying for them is out of the question. "So, what makes y'all want to play with me? This meeting isn't for social reasons." It was time to get to the point. It might push them back a little.

Matthews was ready to handle his part again. "We have no interest in sending you and your wife to jail. We don't want to send Stacy to jail. It's the leader of The Untouchables that we want. Alvin Jones." Matthews and Spanks hoped that they could get Calvin to convince Stacy or his wife to testify against Alvin. They needed a star witness to make the case work. A liar could make a star witness with enough circumstantial evidence.

"I know you ain't thinking about asking me to testify against anyone. That ain't happenin'."

As on cue, Spanks jumped back in. "We've discussed this. We respect that you can't testify." These were just words. If he could get the Vice President to testify against the President, it would all be part of a day's work. "We want you to get your wife or your daughter—preferably Stacy—to testify against Alvin. Stacy is a member of The Untouchables."

Acting insulted would accomplish nothing. They were dead serious and acting a tad desperate. "I can't do that. What you want is for my wife to testify against her daughter. My wife won't testify against Stacy."

Spanks continued, as he threw his legs up on the table. "We just need a witness against Alvin. We are going to put the rest of y'all in the Witness Protection Program."

"Listen. No disrespect, but I ain't testifying. My wife ain't testifying. And Stacy ain't testifying against nobody." In his younger days, he would have jumped out of his seat to make his point.

Spanks had known the answer before the meeting had started. If needed, this would be another strike against Matthews. The cards still had to be played out. "I know you just did nine years. Well, I want you to think about doing a life sentence in a federal penitentiary."

Calvin looked up at the ceiling to be sarcastic. "The statute said ten years. How are you going to get life out of ten years? That's if you can convict me."

"You don't understand that we are going to put you in The Untouchables' conspiracy."

Calvin laughed. "Y'all should let me smoke some of that weed y'all smoking. That's some good shit. How the hell am I going to be in a drug conspiracy and be doing a state bid at the same time?"

His response was expected. It was basically the same way that people who knew a little about the law acted. Matthews took over again. "Did you get it all off your chest?"

"Nah, I didn't. I'm going to sue the shit out of y'all. Y'all act like this is a motherfuckin' game that y'all can play with people's lives."

Spanks stood up. "Now you listen to me. I'm tired of being nice." Spanks hated to be threatened, especially by a defendant. "They call it conspiracy. I'll go to the penitentiary and get a few cats that'll say whatever I want them to say for their freedom or to make parole."

"What the fuck," Calvin murmured.

"Just because you've been giving your daughter advice from the penitentiary is enough to put you in the conspiracy. You remember telling her about the element of surprise and always keep The Man's money right? We got the letters. We even got the one about you telling her that none of the Dees have been a rat."

"You got to be kidding! I haven't seen any drugs. I definitely haven't been selling any."

Spanks laughed. "You have always known that your daughter has been selling heroin, just like you used to do. You are a part of her operation just by giving her advice. I might put your wife in the conspiracy for the hell of it." Matthews was loving the show. Seeing The Untouchables fall meant everything to him. "The Untouchables are going to be charged with the Fifth Street massacre. That means life sentences."

"Listen, man. You can't scare me. I'm going to fight you to the highest court in the land." Calvin had no doubt in his mind that there was no way he could be put in a conspiracy and be held responsible for murders that happened while he was in jail.

"Whatever lawyer you get, he's going to tell you the same thing. You are never going to get a chance to play with your grandson in the free world. He's about to grow up without you, your daughter and your wife." If Spanks couldn't get any assistance, he was going to enjoy using all the dirty tricks that he knew about.

"OK, you said what you had to say. I also said what I had to say. Now lets get to the preliminary hearing and bond hearing." Calvin's plan was to make bond and find out what was really going on.

"I'll do this part," Matthews spoke to Spanks as he put his hand on Spanks' shoulders. Spanks took a seat. "You are not going to make bond."

"Whatever you say." *This fool must think my peeps are broke or something.*

"This is what you can expect to happen. In the morning, we are going to seize all the businesses, houses, bank accounts and cars. We are going to forfeit everything. At your bail hearing, we are going to make sure you don't make bail. You and your wife will be together."

Calvin laughed. He had seldom heard about people not getting a bond.

"Once we deny you bail, we are going to give you a week to change your mind. If you don't, you and your wife are going to be part of a big drug conspiracy. What is your decision?"

"Do what you got to do. Just do what you got to do. I'll die before I help you."

<u>**Chapter Sixteen**</u>

Tuesday, September 5

Stacy was up early. She wanted to catch the morning news to see if anything else was happening with her mother and father. There hadn't been any reason for her to go out at night.

Alvin and Stacy hadn't had a conversation since he had made his proposal. He knew that he had hit her with a bomb. It was best to let her have her space. Them arresting her father, to him, meant that they were about to go all out. Just as he expected, the Feds were digging as hard as they could.

With a half a glass of Hennessy sitting in front of him, Alvin puffed on a cigar. It was almost time for the six o'clock morning news. Stacy sat in her chair across the room. They hadn't missed a news episode since Sunday evening.

Alvin couldn't believe that the police raided Jesse's house and place of business. Alvin looked over at Stacy. He almost said something. Instead, he took a sip of his Hennessy. It was time to do some more serious thinking.

"Mr. Matthews, what else can we expect to happen in The Untouchables case?" the female reporter asked with a big smile. It was an exclusive. Sooner or later she would run a story to the DEA's liking to return the favor.

"My men are also arresting Lisa Sullivan. We have strong

evidence that she's part of Stacy's heroin operation." Matthews made sure that he mentioned Stacy's name.

Stacy yelled out, "Damn." Alvin would have said something then, but he wanted to see the rest of the program.

"Did you say that you are going to convict the rest of The Untouchables *in absentia*?" The Latin term was used to keep the audience's attention. People loved it when they learned a new legal term.

"If we don't catch the rest of The Untouchables, then yes, we are going to try them without them being there."

"Well, there you have it. The DEA is right on top of The Untouchables."

Alvin hit the remote. The television went off. "We got to talk, Stacy."

"Yeah, we got to talk. Why you ain't tell me you are about to die?" She crossed her legs. She wanted answers.

"That isn't important, Stacy. What's important is how we handle this situation. I don't mind you being mad at me." Alvin knew that they were going to slip sooner or later by staying in Philadelphia.

"This is fucked up. They got my mother, son, father, Jesse and my main girl. What's the craziest is that you want me to testify against you. How shit get like this?" Her frustrations had built up. "They are also trying to take all my shit."

There was no argument that Alvin could come up with to say that the entire situation wasn't that bad. "Baby girl, have you thought about what I told you?"

"Well, I've been thinking about there still has to be a rat. If the rat is Tyrone, we just have to find him. Then the Feds won't have a case." So much had happened that Stacy hadn't thought about there had to be a witness to testify. She mainly hadn't been thinking about it because she felt that Quadir was the rat.

"I've thought about that also. My lawyer says that the rat's testimony at the grand jury can be used at trial. Or they can use the rat's statements. A cop will read them."

"So are you basically telling me that they don't need the rat to show up at the trial, and we got no fight in court?" Her thoughts went to whether Lisa and Jesse were going to withstand the pressure that the Feds were going to put on them. She was also hoping that Jesse didn't want revenge because she gave him his ring back.

"Baby girl, we are in a death trap. I want to get you out. I'm going to die anyway."

Stacy frowned. There was too much pain coming at her at once. "I can't believe that you are dying, Alvin."

"It's true, baby. It's the cigars that I've been smoking for forty years." The doctor had been telling him to stop for five years. Alvin took another drag of his cigar. He told the doctor that he needed to smoke to think.

"Damn Alvin, and you still smoking?" Stacy remembered how it was to be addicted to heroin. She wouldn't stop, no matter what anyone told her. "Can't we find a medical center in a foreign country?"

"Once the Feds find out that we've left the country, they are going to have an international manhunt. I don't want you to go through that."

"If I stay here, I'll be getting life sentences. I'm better off on the run."

"I'm going to make it so you can stay here and do your thing. You ain't but a young girl. You can't raise your son from another country or from a jail cell. One of us needs to be here for him."

"So that's what made you start acting soft! Having a son has changed your whole mental." Stacy had been trying to figure out what was up with him. Ever since she had known him, he was willing to fight to the death.

Alvin had to stop and think for a second. "It ain't just that. What good would it be for me to die in prison, or on the run when I can set you free? It's called love, not foolishness." Alvin was worried that he wasn't going to be able to get to her.

"Wouldn't that make me a rat?" Stacy couldn't believe that she was having this conversation, along with all the other things that were going on.

"No, baby girl. You can only be a rat for the government. You are doing it for your son, your people and me. Don't you love me enough to risk your life?"

"You know the answer to that." *He's really serious and trying to sell me on this.*

"I would do the same for you. You ain't going to do a damn thing for the Feds except trick them. I have no plan on letting them win." Alvin really didn't want his son to grow up without his mother. Nor did he want to see Stacy doing a life sentence. It would end up being such a waste.

"There ain't nothin' that I wouldn't do for you. What you are asking me is something that just isn't in my heart. I can't even imagine myself doing something like that." Stacy wanted to shake Alvin to make him stop talking this way.

"Well, you might as well leave the country and plan to be on the run for the rest of your life. I'm going to die in a few months. So you might as well leave without me." He was bluffing about letting her go alone.

"So, it's like that?"

"It's like this. I respect your gangsta. If you tell for them, you a rat. If you tell for me and everybody else, it's love. We'll win. They won't." On that note, Alvin rolled to his bedroom.

* * * *

Tuesday, September 5

Matthews had been on point all morning, waiting for Spanks to come in. If there ever was a time that he wanted to make a fellow officer disappear, it was now.

"I got a deal that will seal The Untouchable case," Matthews said. Spanks had just sat down at his desk. Spanks had plans on doing some serious, though illegal, interrogating. "Santa Claus just dropped a present in our hands that we can't refuse."

Spanks, out of instinct, figured Matthews had been drinking. There was no secret about how badly Matthews wanted to do The Untouchables. "What the fuck are you talking about?"

"We just came up with the best star witness that we could get. When she testifies, Alvin is done." Matthews hadn't had a drink since he had received the proposal. He had been up all night making sure the angles were correct.

"Who the fuck could this witness be?" Spanks humored Matthews. He knew that none of the people that they had in custody knew that much about Alvin. None of them had been that close to him.

"We can get Stacy to do it!"

Spanks stared at him with an intensity that would scare the average man. He stood up from his desk to sniff both sides of Matthews' body. No alcohol lingered. Spanks kept trying to find out what was wrong with Matthews. Their noses were now less than an inch apart.

"We don't even have Stacy in custody. What makes you think she's going to be a rat?" Might as well go along with the game until he could find a weak spot. This might be just what he needed to get rid of Matthews.

"Her lawyer told me that Stacy will testify if we give her transactional immunity." Matthews was tired of smelling Spanks'

aftershave, but Spanks had to be the first one to back down. Showing a sign of weakness would infer that Matthews might be going crazy.

Spanks let the thought run through his mind for a few seconds. He wasn't going to back up just yet. "Do you know what transactional immunity is?" Spanks wanted to see if Matthews was just throwing out words to make a case.

"Yeah, I know what it is. I spoke with the prosecutor." The prosecutor was a young cat that was in Matthews' pocket. "I also looked it up for myself under 18 U.S.C. 6002." This line of questioning was becoming offensive to Matthews.

"So, you want to set Stacy free." Spanks was satisfied with what Matthews had said.

"Not exactly. The deal is that Stacy testifies for everybody to go free, except for Alvin and Tyrone." This was the part that Matthews really didn't want to mention.

Spanks sat down and propped his legs up on his desk. "You must be out of your mind. I know that Lisa or Jesse is going to rat. I can't believe that Jesse is going to do a life sentence for Stacy."

"OK, maybe one of them is going to rat. They still won't be credible witnesses against Alvin. Plus, Alvin is going to leave the state—probably the country—in the next two days." There were too many ways to get out of Philadelphia for them to stop him.

"By the way, when are we supposed to arrest Alvin? What the fuck is he going to do, turn himself in?" Spanks almost forgot about the most important part. He wanted to take a picture with Alvin at the defense table just after the guilty verdict.

"Alvin is going to turn himself in. Alvin wants to get Stacy a new life."

Spanks bowed his head and grabbed his stomach as he started laughing. "Are you fucking out of your mind?"

Matthews had felt the same way when he heard the offer. Jalissa had to tell him four to five times before he accepted it. "Yes, Alvin is going to turn himself in as soon as we give Stacy transactional immunity.

"You know that we can get her later for the same charges," Spanks retorted.

Matthews hadn't exactly thought of this. "They aren't going to go for that. I tried." Telling Spanks the truth wasn't a good option. Matthews had jumped on the deal as soon as he understood what transactional immunity meant. Getting The Untouchables was enough for him. He knew Spanks didn't feel the same.

"So Alvin wants to sacrifice his life for all their lives?" Spanks was now fully convinced that the offer was for real, though it was a little simple. Stacy wasn't the kind to testify. Alvin wasn't the kind to give in. There had to be a catch.

"That's about the gist of it." Matthews' pulse was running at a rapid pace. Sweat beaded up on his forehead. He could see himself only being a few steps away from putting his twenty-year nemesis away. This was the best chance that he had.

"It's hard for me to believe that Stacy and Alvin are going to turn themselves in. There has to be a trick."

"If they turn themselves in, what kind of trick could there be?" Spanks, too, thought that it had to be too simple. Why would Mr. Untouchable just turn himself in to the Feds to get some life sentences? There had to be something missing. "This shit is too easy."

"What the fuck are they going to do—escape?" Matthews could see that his sale was almost complete. "Just suppose that we end up on a manhunt that doesn't turn up anything. This thing could go on for years."

"Well, if it does go on for years, we won't look like fools. Doesn't this seem like it's too good to be true? Plus, we have four potential star witnesses to go with the good witness's testimony. We might not need her."

"OK, let's say they all decide to testify. We still have to find Stacy and Alvin. We know that they're in Philadelphia, but we can't get a lead. They can leave when they like. Alvin has enough money to change their identities and live overseas forever." Convicting Stacy and Alvin without them being at the trial just wouldn't be the same as having them there. To a cop, half the satisfaction was seeing the look on the defendant's face when the verdict was rendered. The other half was when the sentence was given.

Usually, a big drug case took at least nine months of investigation. Still, it was tricky when there were no drugs found. Most of the time, perjured testimony was used to guarantee a conviction. "This just doesn't seem right. I'm going to have to think about this."

"We can have this done in two months, then we can move on to bigger things. This is going to be the biggest feather that either of us can put in our caps." This young fool is going to mess up a wet dream.

"Let's see what happens when we put the heat to Jesse. He'll get scared after Stacy's parents get denied bail. I plan to put lots of pressure on the accountant."

"What can he say about Alvin?"

"He's an accountant. We can get him to lie about laundering Alvin's money. His credibility is great. I can see him on the stand now. The jury will buy whatever he says, especially if he's acting scared." It wasn't time for Spanks to give up on his plan.

"If you listen to me you'll have your picture in the paper with Alvin being sent off to the federal penitentiary. This shit is guaranteed."

Spanks thought about it for a minute. Months of work would be credited to him. This might even get him a promotion. There was the possibility of getting one of those police shows to interview him about how he caught got one of Philadelphia's most notorious criminals. Keeping Alvin and Stacy from going on the run was something that he couldn't ignore. Putting Alvin on the FBI's Most Wanted list would be an embarrassment.

"Damn. You ain't going to give up."

"You know your ass can't ignore the opportunity. Jesse might be in love with that girl." Matthews knew that they were having a relationship.

"We'll see. We'll see. We shall see."

* * * *

The Dees had been sitting in the courtroom for half an hour, but they didn't mind. Spanks hoped that by making them wait together in a big courtroom, they would realize how serious things were about to get. They would be the only ones who didn't know that they were part of a stage show.

Jalissa hated the position that she was in. What was about to go down insulted her sense of justice. She knew there would be no bail. Thinking like a prosecutor, like any good lawyer would do, she knew the angle that would be used to deny the bail. Being truthful about the Feds with a client was seldom a possibility. Selling out wasn't a possibility, either. These feelings made it hard for her to do her job. All she could do was try her hardest, though the denials were like slaps in the face. She always told her clients that things looked good, to keep their hopes up. If she was truthful with them, her clients would think that she went in with a losing attitude. That was something she couldn't risk.

She was surprised to see the Dees sitting in the courtroom. Jalissa knew this meant that they would be first. The young prosecutor Edwin McGregor, who was handling Stacy's case, walked through the side door. It seemed that he had been waiting for her to arrive. Before Jalissa could start a conversation with the Dees, Matthews and Spanks walked through the same door. She waved at all of them. They all nodded their heads.

Calvin wanted to say something to Jalissa to make her feel better. He could see in the Feds eyes that they came to get blood.

"Good morning, Mr. and Mrs. Dee. I hope y'all are well."

"We're OK. Just do your best. We know we are in the belly of the beast," Calvin responded.

No sooner than Spanks and Matthews got to the prosecutor's table, the bailiff came out and stated, "All rise for the Honorable Judge Waverly." A few other lawyers had trickled into the courtroom while Judge Waverly was approaching her bench. A news crew had also come in with them. They set up quickly.

"You may all be seated," Judge Waverly said in a spry voice. "Are the defense and prosecution ready?"

"Yes, Your Honor," they both said at almost the same time. Both were revved up for the fight.

Judge Waverly wanted to say something about them answering so quickly. "We are here this morning for a preliminary hearing and bail hearing for the Dees. They are both charged with money laundering in violation of 18 U.S.C. 1956 and 1957. How do your clients plead?"

"They plead not guilty."

"That was a simple matter. Now is there reason for the court to maintain the charges?"

"Yes, there is," the prosecutor spoke up. "We have financial records to show that the Dees have separately handled large amounts of drug money that they knew was drug money." He smiled. It was one of those cases that mainly required the use of financial records, something really simple.

"Does the defense have anything to say?"

"Yes, the defense does. Your Honor, the prosecutor doesn't have enough proof that the money was gained illegally as proceeds, and that it was used for enhancing criminal activity. I move that these charges be dismissed today." Jalissa knew that what she said was strong and sounded good. She also knew that the prosecutor had a good comeback.

Stacy and Alvin were catching the entire show live. They had expected the Feds to step their game up and to do it in front of the entire city.

"Your Honor, these are the parents of a defendant who was in front of you a few weeks ago for drug charges. Her name is Stacy Dee. Her parents had important roles in Stacy's organization, though they only handled money and gave advice." Proving his case and putting up evidence wasn't needed. As long as the defendants didn't look innocent, his burden had been surpassed.

Judge Waverly liked what she heard. "The defense's motion is denied. Does the defense move for bail?"

Stacy got closer to the television.

"Yes, the defense does move for bail. The defendants are charged with money laundering. With the prosecutor's evidence, the most they'll receive is a ten-year maximum sentence. There aren't any factors that warrant the denial of bail." Jalissa had thought about what was the perfect thing to say. Her response was the problem for which she couldn't find a solution for.

"Does the prosecution have anything to say?"

With a chipmunk smile on his face, the prosecutor stated, "Yes, the prosecution has a few things to say. What the defense said is true and hard to argue with." He started off this way to make what he had to say stand out. "This is an unusual case in which the defendants are in *serious danger*. We have a news paper clipping to substantiate that there is a risk that the Dees may end up getting murdered or kidnapped." The newspaper clipping was about the abduction of Mrs. Dee and her grandson. "This case involves The Untouchables—the most ruthless drug gang in Philadelphia. The defendants should stay in custody for their own safety. The Fifth Street Massacre is attributed to The Untouchables."

The judge's body language indicated that she was impressed. "Does the defense have anything else to say?"

The prosecutor had said exactly what Jalissa was afraid she would hear. "There are no established cases to support the denial of bail. The prosecution has no grounds to believe that Mr. or Mrs. Dee is a threat to the community, or that they may be kidnapped or murdered. If I'm correct, the so-called Untouchables are in hiding and can't be located. I think that at the least, you could place a police car on twenty-four hour surveillance of the Dees. I think that'll serve the purpose for all parties very well." She had winged it. After she finished getting it all out, she felt that she had done well.

The judge took a few seconds to think. Stacy got on her hands and knees. Alvin took a sip, then bit into his cigar and took a big puff. Instantly, he started coughing. His chest hurt with a stinging pain but a big drink eased the pain.

After Judge Waverly pushed her glasses up on her nose, she stated her opinion. "This is a rather close decision and one of a first, sort of to speak. The defendants aren't exactly that dangerous or present a threat to the community, though one of them just got out of prison for murder. I can't even say that there is a real threat of them leaving the city. However, there is a chance that they could end up murdered or kidnapped. This article says that Mrs. Dee and her grandson were kidnapped by The Untouchables. Justice would be obstructed if anything were to happen to the Dees. Bail is denied. The defendants may appeal, if they like." She hit her gavel finalize the decision. By the time an appeal was filed, whether granted or denied, Spanks and Matthews would have done what they needed to do.

Chapter Seventeen

Spanks was the happiest he had been in a long time. It was time to put the pressure on Jesse. *Jesse is a smart black boy. It shouldn't be hard to talk sense to him.* Spanks had Jesse to wait in his office just before the bail hearing started. Jesse was allowed to watch it on television.

"Good morning, Jesse. My name is Special Agent Spanks. I'm the head of the DEA in Philadelphia. I'm here to help you get out of this."

Jesse shook Spanks' hand. They were not using handcuffs in order to make Jesse feel comfortable. Jesse always shook hands with people because that is what he was accustomed to doing. "It's nice to meet you, sir. What is there that you can do for me?"

"You really don't belong here. A smart man like yourself needs to be somewhere with his kids and wife. I can tell that you made a mistake by dealing with a few of the wrong people. All I need is information." Spanks was used to educated people who got caught in a case, and were willing to tell about it before they made it to the police station.

"I don't exactly follow what you are saying. I don't feel that I've committed a crime. I'm just an accountant." Jesse intentionally avoided the subject.

"It seems that you and Stacy know each other rather well.

You've handled a few million dollars of her money. You've also been on a few trips with her. We have enough evidence to give you a life sentence." Most accountants didn't know they could end up getting so much time for just handling drug money. An accountant could easily make an entire case against a defendant.

"You have got to be kidding. There is no way I could get a life sentence for what you just said." There was a smirk on Jesse's face.

"I just had Stacy's parents denied bail. You saw it on television. That's how much power I have. I can make your life miserable. That cell could be your home for a very long time." Spanks hated it when a defendant laughed while he was talking.

Jesse didn't feel like playing games. "I'm not trying to help you. I'm not a rat."

Spanks was surprised to hear him use the term 'rat.' "Stacy doesn't care about you. You might as well tell on her and keep all of her money." Appealing to most people's greed was a successful tactic.

"I'm not telling on the woman I love. I'm just not going to do that." Jesse had intentions of getting Stacy back.

"Did you say that you love her?" Spanks had taken for granted that Jesse could have serious emotions for a street broad.

"Yes, that is correct. I'm trying to marry her."

"I hope you are willing to give up everything for her."

"I am. I am."

Spanks could see that Jesse wasn't an option for being a snitch. A man in love just wasn't going to do certain things.

* * * *

Monday, November 6

In a few hours, Stacy was scheduled to take the stand and testify against a man that she loved, honored and respected to the utmost. There was nothing she wouldn't do for Alvin in the name of the game, without any hesitation. The thought of testifying against him, however, hadn't let her get a good night's sleep since she had agreed to do it. Not even seeing her son every weekend made her feel any better about the situation.

Jesse and her mother, when they visited her, tried to convince her that what she was about to do wouldn't make her a "rat." Jalissa also tried to make her feel better about the situation. Their attempts only made Stacy fall into a deeper depression. On the other side of the coin, if she didn't testify, all of them were going to end up getting convicted. No matter what she did, someone that she loved deeply would end up getting hurt.

If Stacy could stop the hands of time and spend the rest of her life in the FDC, she would have been satisfied. As she got closer and closer to the trial date, she felt worse and worse. Getting it off her mind for a little while was impossible. There was something in every newspaper about The Untouchables and her almost on a daily basis. Even national magazines like *Don Diva, F.E.D.S., Murder Dog, Newsweek, Time,* etc, were running stories and requesting interviews. She did not grant any interviews. The only consolation that she had was that her son was with his grandmother and grandfather, not in a group home. If she had gone on the run, there would be no one in Devon's life who had real love for him, like a blood relative. He was practically the deciding factor that made her agree to the entire deal and testifying. Now that the day had come, she didn't know if she was going to be able to do it.

"Listen Stacy, it isn't going to be that bad." Jalissa had canceled many of her appointments and trial appearances so that she could get Stacy through what was imminent. Jalissa respected Stacy's feelings about being a rat. If the situation had been any different, she would have lost all respect.

"I hear you, girl, but you ain't the one with the spotlight on you. I'll be called a rat forever." Stacy didn't want to be negative with Jalissa. They had been practicing her testimony to the point that she had memorized what she was going to say, word for word. They had to make sure that nothing was left out.

"Just keep in mind that Alvin told you to do this. You ain't doing this for the government. You are doing it for him, and he's sacrificing his life for you and y'all's son." Jalissa had said this to her no less than five times each time she visited.

"It just don't seem like the right thing to do. Alvin is going to have all those life sentences and get the death penalty." She tried to convince Alvin that they should go on the run and kidnap Devon when the time was right, but she couldn't change his mind. Dying was the only thing she could figure that kept him from seeing it her way. He was still the boss anyway.

"Home girl, if you change your mind, it's going to make Alvin look like a fool for sacrificing his life for no reason. That would be disrespectful and an act of disloyalty." Jalissa had been saving this argument for the countdown.

"Damn, yo' ass real slick with those words, lawyer lady. I wish yo' ass was in my shoes to see how this feels," Stacy snapped with sarcasm. They both laughed. Jalissa had hit the button. There was no way that Stacy was going to be disloyal and disrespect Alvin. Making him look like a fool was out of the question.

"Alvin was meticulous with this deal. I must admit that he's a genius. Since he's dying, what could be more true to the game than to give his life for several lives? That's how bad they want to convict him. All you have to do is tell everything, and you and everybody else gets to go free. They don't know that he's dying." A few hours more and Jalissa would be able to walk out of the courthouse with her girl. All Stacy had to do was take the stand and tell it all, live before the world. Jalissa was her moral support.

Spanks and Matthews had become the best of friends since Alvin and Stacy had turned themselves in. On a few occasions, they had even gone out and had drinks together. Spanks didn't mind sharing the spotlight with Matthews. He had already gotten a guarantee that when Alvin was convicted, he would be getting a promotion, bonus and a hefty raise.

They stood side-by-side on the left side of the courtroom, waiting for the camera crews to finish setting up. They didn't want to miss their last chance to get an interview before the trial was to begin.

"Matthews," Spanks said in a friendly tone, "We are going to be some of the most famous cops in the world when this is over. Don't you think it's time that you told me who the rat is that started this case? Or is there a rat?"

Matthews figured that telling him now would not hurt matters. The entire situation was about to be wrapped up and there was nothing Spanks could do to hurt him. "Tyrone is the rat."

Tyrone had arranged a secret meeting with Matthews. After two meetings and a few good statements, Matthews hurried up and went to the grand jury and indicted Stacy. He read Tyrone's statements to them. The only person that Tyrone would give information on was Stacy. Tyrone and Matthews figured Stacy would turn on the crew after mad pressure was put on her. That way, Tyrone really wouldn't be a rat. Tyrone did it because he was going broke and falling off at an accelerated rate. After the case was over, Tyrone was hoping to get twenty-five percent of everybody's property and cash under 19 U.S.C. 1609. When he had heard that a snitch had received a quarter of a million dollars for his services, he could not rest. Getting Quadir's stuff was what enticed him the most.

Tyrone would only tell so much and do so much. There was nothing that would let him testify against Alvin. His pride wouldn't let him go in the Witness Protection Program and his fear of Alvin and Alvin's resourcefulness wouldn't let him risk his family's life. The plan was to let Tyrone get convicted with everybody—then arrange for him to beat the case and leave the country.

Matthews had to accept Tyrone's offer. Tyrone wasn't going to talk to any other officer, and wasn't going to give any information past Stacy. Matthews decided to take it and run. When you have a whole lot of nothing, a little bit of something turns out to be very valuable.

Matthews had moved quickly to put the right people on his team. He understood Tyrone's feelings. Plus, he didn't want to push Tyrone into being a witness because of his fear, and how far he was gone on gambling and drugs. He could easily fuck up a case. It was better to go the other route, even though it was going to be hard as hell to get a conviction unless someone else decided to turn rat and testify. If it hadn't been for Stacy's cell phone, Matthews would have never had any corroborating evidence against The Untouchables. Things had worked out better than Matthews had expected. There was nothing to lose from the beginning. He could have let Stacy go at any time that he felt that he wasn't getting enough. When they kidnapped her mother and son, he knew that was going to push her over the edge and make her make a mistake. It did.

"So, is Tyrone going to testify?" Spanks really didn't care at this stage of the game. Making Matthews look bad was still an option that he wanted to have, just in case.

"No. He won't be able to testify himself. He got murdered last night, just outside a crack house." Matthews had been expecting him to get turned in for the reward. If he had been turned in, Matthews was going to turn on him and convict him after Alvin had been convicted. Might get some more press and another conviction out of the matter.

Spanks just chuckled as he watched members of the press file into the courtroom. "We have Stacy. That is going to be enough. She makes a much better witness than he ever could."

"Still, we are going to read his DEA-6s to the jury." Matthews was looking forward to doing that as part of his testimony.

"Sounds good to me. Let's go outside and see if we can get interviewed one last time." Spanks had really though that Quadir was the C.I. Quadir's power-hungry style had fit the bill of a high-profile rat. Spanks had seen many killers turn into rats at the thought of getting a life sentence. He loved his job.

* * * *

"It's your hot jock, Mr. Jacobs, bringing you the latest. Mr. Untouchable's trial is about to start in fifteen minutes. Philadelphia wants to know if Stacy is going to testify against him. It seems that Stacy may start bangin' 'em in a different way." Since it had been told that Stacy was planning to testify against Alvin, people had started calling her a rat and the radio stations refused to play her records. Many in Philly hated rats, though there were many around.

* * * *

Every news organization from Pennsylvania had reporters in the courtroom. Even CNN, CBS, ABC and a few cable stations had crews on the premises. Some even had cameras mounted in the ceiling. In high-profile cases, the defendant would usually ask that the trial be a closed proceeding. Not in this case. Not one pre-trial motion had been filed by the defense. The press had been welcomed to attend, though they weren't granted any interviews. The press had dubbed Alvin as one of the most sophisticated and dangerous drug dealers of all time. Never had anyone heard about a drug organization that was able to operate for decades without the police knowing the identities of the members. Everybody wanted to know how he had made it happen. The biggest piece of information that the media could come up with was that Alvin had done a bid in the Pennsylvania penitentiary. Alvin had become an instant worldwide celebrity. Spanks and Matthews didn't mind because they were credited with bringing him in.

Alvin had spent most of his time reading newspapers, books and magazines and listening to the radio. He had been placed on the seventh floor of FDC. No other inmates got to see him or hear his voice. There were no other inmates on his tier. Having Alvin in population with the rest of the inmates at FDC Philadelphia wasn't going to happen. Alvin knew too many people and had way too much influence. Naturally, Alvin had to have his Hennessy and cigars. On a few occasions, Spanks would send in a guard to confiscate Alvin's goodies. In less than a day, Alvin would have a fresh supply and whatever else he wanted. Spanks gave up after the third try. There was no way for him to monitor every cop that went to Alvin's cell.

Deep inside, Spanks wanted to make Alvin suffer. There was nothing he could really do to Alvin, for Alvin had chosen his own path. Alvin would just stare at Spanks when Spanks would try to verbally rouse him. Most of the time, Alvin's sardonic grin and nonchalant cigar smoking frustrated Spanks. Spanks was really trying to figure out what was on Alvin's mind. Why would Alvin take all those life sentences and the death penalty when he could have just went on the run? Spanks only knew for sure that Alvin wasn't going to escape and that there was going to be a trial.

Alvin's lawyer wheeled him into the courtroom. They had to come through the underground tunnel. Alvin wore a black pinstriped suit. The way that his legs were crossed and the way that he dangled a cigar in his fingers made the news crews wonder if Alvin was out of his mind or something. By the grin on Alvin's face, if a person didn't know it, they would have assumed that he was going to a party or a similar festive occasion.

Matthews, Spanks and the young prosecutor hated how the press made such a fuss over Alvin. They were at the defense table. If it weren't for the four-man U.S. Marshal escort, the press would have been right on top of Alvin to get a comment or two. A few hollered out on general principle. There was nothing to lose. Alvin just kept smiling. His lawyer just kept pushing and smiling.

After Alvin was at the defense table, the marshals let the crowd into the courtroom. Many of them had been waiting for hours. The smart ones knew that only so many people were going to be allowed in and got here early. Buying tickets wasn't a possibility; anyone from the public was allowed in. There was a line all the way around the block. Most were going to be turned around and would have to opt for seeing it on television. There were many bets that Stacy wasn't going to testify. For weeks, no matter what happened, people would be talking. Many wanted to be right in the midst of 'hood history. Philadelphia's most notorious was about to stand trial, with Philadelphia's most Gangsta Bitch about to take the stand against him. All else was secondary.

"All rise," the bailiff called at so that Judge Waverly could make her entrance. Judge Waverly wanted to say a few slick things to Alvin to figure out what he was trying to accomplish. Her social friends had been worrying her about Alvin since the day he turned himself in. They wanted to know what was the catch. They had never heard of anyone volunteering to take a few life sentences, and maybe the death penalty, then act like it was nothing. Being on international television caused the judge to be on her best behavior. She was going to do the least she had to do.

Judge Waverly looked out over crowd for a few seconds. Never had she seen her courtroom so packed. Every seat was filled and many were standing up in the back. All eyes were on her, and there was complete silence.

"Bring the jury in," she ordered. The jury had been picked on Sunday. Alvin had waived his appearance. Who was on the jury wasn't significant. Though the trial was to be as simple as it could get, the prosecution wasn't taking any chances. They made sure that none of the jurors were fans of Alvin or other criminals. Many of the jurors they picked were related to people in law enforcement. It wouldn't be an issue on appeal because all appellate rights had been waived with the deal. Jury picking couldn't have been a more fun process for the prosecution.

At ten forty-five, the trial was all set to begin. Edwin McGregor called his first witness to the stand: Matthews, the man who knew more about The Untouchables than anyone else. Matthews was ready and loving every bit of attention that he was getting. It had taken years of torment and anguish. Finally, he was going to resurrect himself and his reputation and fulfill his lifetime ambition—to stop The Untouchables.

Before Matthews began his testimony, Alvin motioned for his attorney to hand him a pencil and a writing pad. The marshals and Spanks watched every move that Alvin made. Many of the viewers in the audience were undercover police officers and they all took note also. Spanks was not about to let the courtroom get bum rushed by fanatics trying to break Alvin out or anyone else. Spanks wanted to go take the pad and pencil. His instincts were screaming, but prudence told him that he would be totally embarrassed on international television. That wouldn't look good at all. It was only a pencil and a writing pad. What harm could all of that do?

Alvin held the pencil poised over the pad while he was waited for Matthews to start testifying. The jury had a keen eye on Alvin. They had heard all the other things that everybody had heard. It was impossible for them not to. They had to wonder what he was up to.

Matthews' testimony started with the statements that he had taken from Tyrone. Now all of Philadelphia knew that Tyrone was the one who started the case. Many in the courtroom started making noise. There had been a great debate in the street. Judge Waverly banged on her gavel to get order. This was one of the few times that she would have to do so.

Chapter Eighteen

"Yo, it's your hot jock, Mr. Jacobs, hollerin' at you with the latest." He had stopped playing a track to do an emergency news bulletin. "We now know who caused The Untouchables to catch a federal case. Special Agent Mark Matthews testified that Tyrone came to him and started giving information. That's right, Tyrone was the one who started the case against The Untouchables. The question is, whether Stacy is going to finish the case."

The entire city was on pause. It was almost unbelievable. What made Tyrone turn, was what everyone wondered. Some still questioned it. If they weren't watching it on television, they were definitely listening out for the latest on the radio.

* * * *

As Matthews testified, Alvin wrote things down on his pad. Many of the camera crews that had overhead cameras tried to zoom in to get what he was writing. They couldn't tell because he kept his left hand over the pad. Spanks was getting mad because he wanted to see Alvin stressing just a little bit. Instead, Alvin acted as if he was a reporter instead of the defendant about to get the federal death penalty or a bunch of life sentences. Snatching the pad and pencil away was at the forefront of Spanks' thoughts.

The jury took note that Alvin acted more like a reporter than a man on trial. With the gruesome details Matthews gave them, they couldn't help but to keep looking over at Alvin. Matthews was sure that he didn't miss any details. Without any objections from the defense, Matthews was allowed to make himself look like a victim that had been tortured for years just because he wanted justice. The jury was falling for it. Alvin and his attorney sat there like it was their stand-in role in a movie script.

Judge Waverly was awed by the event. She was looking at a lawyer that was known for his tenacious objections and aggressive cross-examinations. There hadn't been one objection yet. She didn't expect this. The young prosecutor was having a field day and stirring the emotions of the jury with his questions. If there were objections, Judge Waverly felt that she would have been compelled to agree by sustaining them. Most awesome to her was how the defendant was acting. She was used to defendants putting up a fight, even when they knew that the evidence was overwhelming. No one could have told her that she would participate in a trial like this. She really had something that she could talk to the girls about. Just a small objection for show would have made her feel better about the integrity of the trial and court.

There were no objections. Neither Alvin nor his attorney made a comment while Matthews was testifying. They just sat there. Matthews was beaming and gawked at Alvin as he got off the stand. Alvin acted like he wasn't taking notice of what was happening. To everyone's surprise, Alvin motioned for his lawyer to hand him an envelope. What Alvin had written on the first two pages was placed in the envelope. Some of the jury members wanted to laugh at the smile on Alvin's face as he licked the envelope. They could sense that he was slighting the government. Spanks wanted to go grab the letter that much more. Alvin got a stamp from his lawyer and placed it on the envelope. The letter was placed in the lawyer's briefcase. Spanks would never attempt to harass an officer of the court by pressing the lawyer to let him read the letter, especially after it had been sealed and stamped. This meant that he would be tampering with the U.S. mail.

"Did you see what Alvin did with that envelope and paper while you were on the stand?" Spanks asked Matthews as he approached the prosecution's table.

"Listen, man. He couldn't have made a nuclear bomb with a pencil, pad and envelope," Matthews responded with a smile on his face.

"I know Alvin is up to something. I just know it."

"Just relax. Before the day is over, he'll be convicted and on his way to Colorado to a lockdown facility, where he will never make human contact until it's time for him to die." Matthews loved what was happening and couldn't believe that he had just experienced every cop's testimonial dream—to testify against a defendant in a free manner without objections and cross-examinations. Cops hated getting caught up in lies.

More history had just been told on The Untouchables in two hours than had been told for thirty years. It was like a prologue, being that Matthews could only testify to the supposed activities. The murders, the corruption, the violence, the kidnappings, and the drug dealing were things Matthews hadn't exactly witnessed first hand. The only inside accounts he could testify to were related to what Tyrone had told him. Still, it was a great foundation. It wasn't a secret that Matthews' testimony was colored by his lifelong desire to bring The Untouchables to their knees. Incomplete as his testimony was, it left the world wanting to hear more from a witness that was on the inside. Judge Waverly was so caught up with suspense that she skipped the lunch break. There were no objections. They couldn't wait for Stacy.

Jalissa came through the side door first. Stacy was right behind her. Both were dressed in matching black outfits, again looking like sisters. Every camera and every eye was on them. No one was exactly sure of what to think or expect. Alvin was smiling and waiting to make eye contact with Stacy.

Things were just like Jalissa had been telling Stacy. Stacy did her best to ignore the crowd, the jury and the cameras. She prayed to herself that her mother wasn't letting her son watch this. In her peripheral vision she saw Alvin. Eye contact would be made when she got on the witness stand. She didn't look at him until she was sworn in and seated in the witness box. Alvin was still smiling to make her feel comfortable.

None of the jury members could take their eyes off Stacy. They knew who she was because of her pictures in the media. They had to ask themselves if this young, innocent-looking girl had really been involved with such mayhem and violence. Her testimony couldn't come quick enough.

Jalissa was at the defendant's table and ready to get down to business. She was waiting for Stacy to make eye contact. It had been agreed in the contract that Jalissa would solicit her testimony.

Stacy couldn't believe how packed the courtroom was. Her thoughts of running off the witness stand and saying "fuck it" couldn't get out of her head. She felt a little better when Alvin lipped to her that it was OK. She was as ready as she was going to get after taking two minutes to look at the crowd and jury.

Judge Waverly was loving it. She didn't think Stacy was going to testify against Alvin. The judge could see that there were some serious feelings between them. As a woman, she understood how much anxiety Stacy was going through. She could see it on her face. The suspense was just as good to Judge Waverly as it was to the rest of the world.

"Would you please state your name for the court," Jalissa said to start things off. Her first goal was to get Stacy comfortable and talking.

"My name is Stacy Dee." Jalissa had told her that once she got started, that it would be easy. So far, that wasn't true. Alvin helped push her along by waving his pencil.

Matthews was saying to himself that he just needed her to go a little bit further to get a good flow going. A conviction was imminent. There was no way for them to lose. Spanks fidgeted in his seat.

"Are you a member of any drug organizations?"

"Yes. I'm a member of The Untouchables." She kept telling herself that she was doing it for Alvin. It was an act of love.

"Do you know the defendant who's on trial?"

This was the point of no return. She looked over at Alvin again. The jurors kept taking note that Alvin and Stacy were making a lot of eye contact. They wondered what was really going on. If Alvin had made the wrong facial expression, she would have jumped off the stand. He nodded his head and waved his pencil to urge Stacy, all the while with a smile on his face.

Matthews was smiling. He could see that it would soon be over. Spanks had his eyes on Alvin. Writing on a tablet can't be that harmful, can it, he kept asking himself. He tried to keep his anger down. He was mad at how Alvin was running the show.

"Yes, I know the defendant." Her words came out slowly. It was not easy for her. They barely heard her.

"Would you repeat that," Judge Waverly requested.

"Yes, I know the defendant." Stacy was louder.

"Would you tell us the defendant's name and how you know him?" Just get her past this point and she'll be able to flow with it.

Stacy looked at Alvin and took a big swallow. He nodded and waved his pencil again. He was acting more like a coach than a man on trial for murders and drug charges and facing the death penalty.

"His name is Alvin Jones. And he's the leader of The Untouchables." Before she said it, she reminded herself that she wasn't doing it for the government.

Matthews and Spanks hung onto every word. Stacy testified from twelve o'clock until four o'clock. She told them everything. Alvin sat there as if listening to a story. He was glad that it was Stacy telling the first account of how he did things. Matthews and Spanks still hated that Alvin was acting like he was having so much fun. There was nothing that they could do. They were about to get the conviction that they bargained for. If things had gone any other way, they would have only been able to convict the Dees and Jesse for money laundering.

Jalissa made sure that Stacy didn't miss a thing. Judge Waverly and the audience were spellbound. It was something they had never witnessed and never thought would be possible. It seemed like what Stacy was telling them was more like something that would come out of a book. Philadelphia felt a blow to the stomach. People in the streets were saying that Stacy had turned into a rat. They really couldn't believe it. Some of them even turned off their television sets.

Stacy ended her testimony with how the Fifth Street Massacre went down. Though she was relieved that it was over, she felt an empty feeling in her stomach. Making things worse was the smile on Alvin's face. She couldn't figure out why Alvin was smiling so much. Judge Waverly was spellbound. Still, there were no objections or cross-examination. No one knew if Stacy was finished or if there was more. They just couldn't believe what they had just heard.

Jalissa remained standing by the witness box to see if her friend was OK. She was worried about how Stacy was going to feel afterward. Jalissa had coached her and pushed her through all of her testimony.

"I believe the defense rests," Jalissa announced to the court. She had to say something to make the thing final.

"Yes, the prosecution rests," the young prosecutor jumped up and shouted. He had played his easy role.

Matthews and Spanks looked over at Alvin to see if his facial expression was still the same. To their surprise, he was smiling and tapping the pencil eraser against his front teeth. This really pissed them off.

As Matthews and Spanks stood, Alvin wrote something on his writing pad in big letters. Now Spanks really wanted to run over and take the pencil and pad. Stacy was still on the stand and wondering what they were about to do. Her first instinct was to protect Alvin. Spanks started walking toward the defense table. He couldn't take it anymore.

Alvin's expression changed to one of seriousness. He and Spanks eyed each other with deadly stares. The audience and the cameras turned their attention to them. Spanks was redder than hot lava coming out of a volcano. He felt disrespected. He had to do something.

Alvin stuck the pencil eraser in his mouth and pulled it out without breaking eye contact with Spanks. With the smoothness of a swan, Alvin put the top of the pencil in his mouth and tilted his head. The pencil was sticking straight up in the air. Swallowing the cyanide tablet disguised as a pencil eraser, Alvin held onto his chest. He began to have a seizure as he foamed at the mouth. Everyone in the courtroom stood in shock. They couldn't believe their eyes. A minute later, Alvin was dead.

"What did he just do," Spanks yelled out. "I know that man just didn't die on me!" Spanks grabbed Alvin by the collar and started shaking him. The entire courtroom was on its feet, except for Stacy and Judge Waverly.

Stacy realized what Alvin wanted to accomplish and had accomplished. Alvin had played the government to the max. They thought they were going to take his life. Instead, he chose his own destiny and made sure that she hadn't lost her chance at a full life. She had played her part by testifying. By the contract, they had to set her free. She told them about every crime that she had ever committed. Transactional immunity meant that she couldn't be convicted. She began to feel better. She was happy that the joke was on Matthews and Spanks.

Matthews was about to go into shock. Alvin had outsmarted him again. Years of work had been for nothing. Nobody was going to jail. Nobody was going to get convicted. Everybody that was still alive from the case was going to go free. There would be no celebration for a guilty verdict. He was embarrassed, and there was nothing he could do about it. Mr. Untouchable would go down in history at his expense. Matthews sat back down in his chair and started mumbling to himself.

Judge Waverly just shook her head. History had gone down in her courtroom. It was funny to her how Spanks was trying to make the paramedics bring Alvin back to life. She was thoroughly amused. She was also thoroughly curious. She came from behind her bench. Spanks was still arguing with the paramedics to do something, urging them do something, anything. They just continued to strap Alvin to a stretcher. Judge Waverly picked up Alvin's writing pad. It read: STILL UNTOUCHABLE. She ordered Spanks to read it.

"Lock Stacy up," he yelled to the marshals.

Chapter Nineteen

"This is your hot jock, Mr. Jacobs, bringing you the latest. Mr. Untouchable committed suicide right after Stacy finished testifying. To go with that, I have a tape that Mr. Untouchable made for the city to hear. Y'all need to check this out."

"If you are listening to this tape, it means I, Alvin Jones, Mr. Untouchable, have given my life so that Stacy Dee can have hers. I want the city and the world to know that Stacy isn't a rat. She has never been a rat. And she will never be a rat." The entire city had come to a crashing halt. It was all beginning to make sense. "Stacy did what I told her to do because she is loyal. I gave my life so she could have her life. She's too young to be on the run or doing life sentences. Let it be known that Stacy isn't a rat, and I'm still untouchable."

Many in the streets started celebrating. The government had been tricked by a cat that was true to the game all the way till death. They had no choice but to respect all of that which had went down. Nothing more could be asked of a gangster.

* * * *

Spanks sat in his office trying to figure out what there was that he could do. Matthews wasn't any help. All Matthews could do or say was, "We can't touch him. He's untouchable." They had to take him to an asylum. Convicting Alvin *in absentia* was an option that would make him look desperate. All the news channels reported how "Mr. Untouchable cheated the DEA out of a conviction and sentence." There would be no raise, no promotion, no bonus. Instead of explaining to his superiors what went wrong, Spanks opted to resign and move out of the country.

The young prosecutor was told to continue to pursue the cases against Stacy, her family and Jesse. They refused to let Stacy go. Jalissa immediately filed a writ of mandamus to the Third Circuit Court of Appeals.

Stacy was going to miss Alvin. Still, she had no choice but to be grateful to him. He had done what he had done to give her life back without having to worry about going to jail or getting murdered. She also wished that it all could have been done so that he would have been with her. Philadelphia had started showing her love again. All knew that she wouldn't have turned on Alvin, no matter the consequences. She was once again Philly's Gangsta Bitch.

The Third Circuit Court made a quick decision. They made the attorney's office turn Stacy loose and drop all the indictments against her and everyone else. They stated that Stacy had totally fulfilled her obligations. It wasn't her fault that a conviction wasn't acquired. They had the option of convicting *in absentia*.

Jesse had arranged for Stacy to be picked up by a limousine. Jalissa and Stacy had a girls' day at the beauty salon and mall. Many people welcomed Stacy back to the streets when they saw her. Stacy and Jalissa laughed, joked and shopped to their hearts' content on Jesse's gold American Express Card.

Jesse and Stacy met up later so they could do their thing.

"I never doubted that all things were going to be all right," Jesse said as they toasted champagne glasses. They were at the Radisson's five-star restaurant.

"So that's what you were thinking the entire time." Stacy was using all of her resistance to keep from jumping him. Sexing

Jesse until he could do nothing but call out her name was the only thing on her mind. Getting a few orgasms is what she also wanted for herself.

"I'm ready to be a father to your son." He and Devon had gotten to know each other really well. Jesse had a plan.

Stacy wasn't expecting that. She was anxious to see her son and surprise him. What Jesse was saying sounded really good. "And what else do you have on your mind?" *The setting is perfect. He had better get this right.*

"I made sure you wouldn't have to ever worry about looking over your shoulder. You are my woman. I'm going to make sure that you are always protected. I put two in Tyrone's head."

This bought a smile to her face. "Keep talking." *You had better say what I want you to say.*

Jesse reached across the table and grabbed her hand in such a smooth fashion she had barely noticed. "I still want you to marry me." He had the ring in his other hand and held it up to the candlelight.

"Do you think that you could handle it?" Stacy was trying to let him know that her demands and standards were high.

"I can handle anything that you can put on the table." He slid the ring on her finger. "Will you marry me?"

"I couldn't wait for you to ask me again." This time she didn't feel nervous at all. "Yes, I will." They flew to Vegas the next morning after a night of non-stop sex, and did the damn thing.

There was nothing for Stacy to complain about. She had her life back. She had a son and a good husband to be his father. She would never tell Devon or Jesse that Alvin was the biological father. Why take the risk of a man being insecure? Her mother and father were back together. Radio stations all over the country put her single, "I'm Bangin' 'Em" into heavy rotation.

Interscope Records signed her to a lucrative deal and hooked her up with Dr. Dre. There was nothing that could go wrong.

A few weeks later Jalissa brought her a letter that Alvin had written her. Jalissa had been instructed to wait until Stacy had gotten herself settled before giving her the letter.

Dear Baby Girl,

I'm writing this letter while Matthews is giving his testimony. There is nothing he can do to me because I chose my destiny.

I lived my life to the fullest and I did the damn thing just like I wanted to. I want you to live your life to the fullest. I hope you marry Jesse. That's why I'm giving my life, so that you can have your life.

I know it's going to be hard for you to understand and go through. I couldn't expect any less. You have remained true to the game.

I must confess something to you. I wasn't really dying. I told you that to make you feel better and make you testify. I had to do all I could to make you testify. It was hard to convince you.

I'm still untouchable. Take care of our son!!!

Stacy was touched. His writing to her about why he did it gave it an extra significance and bigger impact. Tears welled up in her eyes. Stacy didn't know what to say or think. It was definitely the greatest act of love that she had ever experienced. All she could do was write a song about it.

Soon it came time for her to do her first concert. The album had been released two months earlier and was doing well, almost platinum. Her girl Lisa was her road manager. Jesse was her manager. Her mother and father ran the businesses and properties that Alvin had left to her and Devon. Everybody in the city was at the concert. The entire arena was sold out. She had just finished doing her already hot single, "I'm Bangin' Em." The crowd was going crazy. They knew every word.

"This song is dedicated to Mr. Alvin Jones, Mr. Untouchable. As y'all already know, it was produced by Dr. Dre."

Philadelphia was already familiar with the song. When that one-of-a- kind gangster beat came on, everybody started bobbing their heads and singing the chorus.

"There will never be another (No)

What a hell of a brother (Oh)

No one else is capable

He's Untouchable"

"Can't nobody do it
Ain't no need to try
He was true to the game
We all saw him die
The police couldn't touch him
'Cause they did know his name
How he put it down
Was a hell of a thang
They couldn't put him in jail
Nor touch his money
He tricked Matthews
Made him look like a dummy
A straight-up genius

And ahead of his time

With a heart of gold

He didn't have to die

But he did it for me

So I could have a life

Nothing else could

Have been more right

We could have split

And never came back

He wanted more for me

I love him for that

We did the thing and

I was willing to die

I'm that gangsta bitch

That's part of the life

He put down a plan

That was indestructible

He chose his path

He's Mr. Untouchable"

> *"There will never be another (No)*
>
> *What a hell of a brother (Oh)*
>
> *No one else is capable*
>
> *He's Untouchable."*

The Ultimate Gangsta Bitch went triple platinum in less than six months.

Stacy

ORDER FORM

Triple Crown Publications
2959 Stelzer Rd.
Columbus, Oh 43219

Name: _____

Address: _____

City/State: _____

Zip: _____

		TITLES	PRICES
		Dime Piece	$15.00
		Gangsta	$15.00
		Let That Be The Reason	$15.00
		A Hustler's Wife	$15.00
		The Game	$15.00
		Black	$15.00
		Dollar Bill	$15.00
		A Project Chick	$15.00
		Road Dawgz	$15.00
		Blinded	$15.00
		Diva	$15.00
		Sheisty	$15.00
		Grimey	$15.00
		Me & My Boyfriend	$15.00
		Larceny	$15.00
		Rage Times Fury	$15.00
		A Hood Legend	$15.00
		Flipside of The Game	$15.00
		Menage's Way	$15.00

SHIPPING/HANDLING (Via U.S. Media Mail)   **$3.95**

TOTAL   **$**_____

FORMS OF ACCEPTED PAYMENTS:

Postage Stamps, Institutional Checks & Money Orders, all mail in orders take 5-7 Business days to be delivered.

ORDER FORM

Triple Crown Publications
2959 Stelzer Rd.
Columbus, Oh 43219

Name: _____

Address: _____

City/State: _____

Zip: _____

	TITLES	PRICES
	Still Sheisty	$15.00
	Chyna Black	$15.00
	Game Over	$15.00
	Cash Money	$15.00
	Crack Head	$15.00
	For the Strength of You	$15.00
	Down Chick	$15.00
	Dirty South	$15.00
	Cream	$15.00
	Hood Winked	$15.00
	Bitch	$15.00
	Stacy	$15.00
	Life Without Hope	$15.00

SHIPPING/HANDLING (Via U.S. Media Mail)   **$3.95**

TOTAL $_____

FORMS OF ACCEPTED PAYMENTS:
Postage Stamps, Institutional Checks & Money Orders, all mail in orders take 5-7 Business days to be delivered.